THE RIFT

A BOLINGBROOK BABBLER STORY
BOOK 2

WILLIAM BRINKMAN

For the latest news about William Brinkman and the Bolingbrook Babbler stories, subscribe at https://bolingbrookbabbler.com/mailing-list

Praise for the Bolingbrook Babbler Stories

Pathways to Bolingbrook:

"Two smart women trying to survive in difficult times. *Pathways to Bolingbrook* captures your imagination and leaves you wanting to know what happens next. Can't wait for the publication of the novel. Well worth reading." — Amazon reviewer.

"This is a very short introduction to what is sure to be an entertaining series, if just for ONE THING: Iowa is not boring." — Amazon reviewer.

"Keep reading. Keep writing, Mr. Brinkman, and all the best with your Anti-Psychic Kitty Press. Breathlessly waiting for your next publication. Six stars!" — Amazon reviewer.

A Fire in the Shadows:

"A thrilling 'vampire' fantasy packed full of twists, turns – and danger!" — Wishing Shelf.

"This was a fast-paced and exhilarating supernatural and sci-fi YA fantasy! The world-building and mythos that the author built into this series were evident immediately." — Author This was a fast-paced and exhilarating supernatural and sci-fi YA fantasy! The world-building and mythos that the author built into this series were evident immediately." — Anthony Avina, author

"I have never read a book so fast before! It sucks you in from the very first sentence. I can't wait to read more books from this author." — Goodreads reviewer.

The Rift:

"A richly written novel filled with memorable characters. Highly recommended!" — The Wishing Shelf.

"A quick, easy and interesting read that had good writing, a good storyline and well developed characters." — Goodreads reviewer.

"Every new development in the story surprised me and -- there are weredeer!I don't usually read fantasy or sci-fi, but this book made me want to take another look at the genre. I highly recommend it!" — Amazon reviewer.

"*The Rift* is a wild adventure, sprinkled with humor, duplicitous characters, and extraterrestrials. You never know who is working for the good of mankind or creating a rift in the world." — Amazon reviewer.

To my wife, who has a real humanist heart.
In memory of Robert Habenstein, whose knowledge,
courage, and heart guided many.

Prologue

"The world is all there is, and all we need."
—Preamble to the International Ethical Union's First Manifesto

"The Truth is unbelievable."
—Motto of the *Bolingbrook Babbler*

Tom Larsen's eyes widened. Glancing towards the entrance of the Jewel-Osco, he saw his parents overtake a slow-moving person blocking the automatic door. He pointed excitedly towards the newsstand.

"Mom! Dad! The new *Babbler* is here!"

As his father mouthed "Indoor voice," Tom's attention returned to the week's edition of the *Bolingbrook Babbler*. Since moving to Bolingbrook, IL, Tom had read every issue, his mother helping with words he didn't understand According to the *Babbler*, Bolingbrook was full of wonders. Half-human weredeer lived in the forest preserves

Clow International Airport was a front for the world's largest urban UFO base; vampire gangs roamed the neighborhoods at night. Why, Tom wondered, did he ever dread leaving Chicago? Bolingbrook really was the galaxy's most important suburb.

This week's edition featured a blurry photo of a UFO hovering by one of Bolingbrook's water towers. *MAYOR FORCES MARTIAN COLONIES TO CANCEL INVASION*, the headline screamed at Tom, who pivoted towards his parents. "Please?"

"Tom," his mother said calmly. "I'll buy you a copy, but first, you'll have to help us with the groceries."

Tom looked back at the issue. "I wanna know what happened."

"It tells you what happened," his father sighed. "The Martians decided not to invade."

"Martian *colonists*," corrected Tom. "The strongest empire in the galaxy."

"Tom," his mother replied. "The sooner we finish shopping, the sooner you'll know." Tom's father bristled.

Tom pined back at the *Babbler* as his mother clasped his hand, and followed when he felt her gentle tug. Soon, Tom was quietly helping his parents while daydreaming about the issue. *Shopping takes so, so long.*

Several long minutes later, as they reached the cereal aisle, Tom stopped and realized his mouth was agape. In front of him stood a familiar man with graying red hair, wearing a white polo shirt with tan slacks. Noticing Tom, he looked down and smiled.

"Hello there," said the man.

Tom froze for a few moments and then reached back with one arm. When he felt his mother's leg, he tapped it, then pointed at the man.

"Don't point," Tom heard his mother say. "Oh. Good day, Mayor Clark."

"Please," the mayor replied. "Call me Robert. Everyone does."

Tom lowered his arms as his father approached.

"I'm Michelle Larsen," his mother replied. "This is my son Tom."

"And I'm her husband, Jason."

"Robert Clark." Robert confidently shook hands with Tom's parents, then kneeled to face Tom. "Hello, Tom. Don't worry. I don't bite kids."

Tom nervously giggled.

"Have we met before?"

Tom shook his head. "I've read about you in the *Babbler*."

Robert's face seemed to brighten. "Oh, really? What did they write?"

"You're the most important mayor in the galaxy."

Robert grinned and nodded. "That's what they wrote?"

"Yes. And you saved Bolingbrook from the Martian Colonies."

"Tom," said Jason. "You can't say that to the mayor."

"It's okay," interrupted Robert. "The *Babbler* has been around since the village was incorporated in the sixties. Every mayor's had to deal with it."

"Thank you for saving us," said Tom.

"No need to thank me," Robert replied. "It's my job."

"When I get home, I'm going to read how you beat the Martian fleet."

"I didn't beat the fleet," Robert said, looking around as if to make sure no one was listening. "Here's what I really did. The Martian Colonial ambassador demanded I surrender. Now, most mayors would have surrendered. But I looked the ambassador straight in the eye and said, 'I am Mayor Robert Clark, and I am Bolingbrook.' Once she realized I wasn't afraid of her, she backed down."

Tom gasped.

Robert stood up, and Tom's eyes followed him. "The rest," said Robert, "you'll have to read for yourself."

Michelle placed her hands on Tom's shoulders and pulled him closer. "I'm sorry if—"

Robert shook his head. "I have a daughter and a niece. I understand."

Robert turned his attention to Jason. "Jason Larsen. You're the new resident who wrote in about Americana Estates." Jason nodded. "You're the first resident to email me. I'm impressed."

"Thought it'd get your attention."

Robert chuckled. "It did."

"You really think there's a benefit to taxpayers funding a luxury golf course and upper-class homes?"

"Absolutely," Robert replied. "We think unconventionally here in Bolingbrook."

Michelle quickly stepped between Robert and Jason. "You know, Robert, we really need to finish shopping. Maybe you two can exchange emails about this?"

"Robert," asked Tom. "Can I tell Dad about the secret supercomputer?"

"Let me," Robert replied. "You can tell him about the men in blue."

***

As Michelle entered the kitchen, balancing a large pizza box, she heard Tom repeatedly yelling no. Tossing the box on the counter, she followed Tom's voice down to the basement, where she saw Jason and Tom on the couch, Tom's Ethical Sunday School drawings littering the floor. Jason was hugging Tom and patting him on the back.

"I'm sorry," said Jason. "I know it hurts, but you're going to be okay. I still love you."

"What happened?" Michelle asked as she approached.

"I told him the truth about the *Babbler*."

Michelle gasped. "You didn't. You should have waited for me."

"Reese's package arrived, so I thought now was a good time. I didn't expect this." Jason picked up one of the pictures from the floor. "I had to stop him from tearing it to pieces."

Jason handed the picture to Michelle. It showed a boy with a rock sitting in a cave, watched by a green dragon with yellow teeth.

Tom stood and hesitantly stepped towards Michelle. "Mom?" he asked, trembling. "I'm the stupid boy with the rock." Tom burst into tears. Michelle rushed up to him and embraced him tightly, humming his favorite song.

Jason reached for one of the three remotes on the coffee table. "We need to show it to him."

"I still say you should have waited."

Jason pressed a button, then stood up. "Well, you're here now. I'll get it ready."

"Let's talk about the stable boy and the rock," said Michelle, sitting down with Tom on the couch. "As I recall, there was a little boy who was brought to a dragon's lair."

"Dogma the dragon." Tom pointed to the dragon in the picture, who sat atop a pile of rulebooks.

Michelle nodded. "He looks scary. Good job." Tom smiled. "Now, the boy was scared, but he was also thirsty. So he asked the dragon for a cup of water. Dogma said no, and told the boy if he was thirsty, he could squeeze water out of a rock. So the boy squeezed and squeezed, but no water came out. Dogma told the boy that if he believed, it would. So the boy squeezed and squeezed and believed and believed. Still, no water came out."

"Until the knight of truth appeared and chased Dogma away."

Michelle nodded, picking up another of Tom's drawings, which showed a knight holding a glowing sword. "You drew that very well."

"Thanks," Tom replied.

"So the knight told the boy there was no water in the rock, and the boy rued his foolishness."

"I don't want to be foolish."

Jason sat down with them. "Neither did the boy. He vowed to slay all the dragons of deception and asked the knight of truth to teach him how to vanquish them. The knight took him under his wing. The boy studied and trained for a long time, till one day he became a knight of truth himself, and he was never fooled again."

Michelle frowned. "That's your dad's version."

"It's the best version. Don't you agree, Tom?" Tom nodded vigorously. "Good. Because a very special movie just arrived." Jason picked up what looked like a CD. Tom's jaw dropped as he remembered the giant LaserDiscs his grandparents still owned. "It's about a wise old man who fights dogma," Jason continued.

"With a sword?"

"With magic."

Jason stood up and inserted the disc into the DVD player, then joined Michelle and Tom back on the couch. He placed an arm around Tom's shoulders and pressed play. On-screen, a magician with thick, professionally styled hair and a neatly trimmed snowy white beard appeared behind a desk.

"You know what the best part is?"

Tom shook his head.

"He's real."

Chapter 1

"A scientific skeptic is a person who applies the methods of science and reason to all claims of fact, prefers evidence to feelings, questions all beliefs, and strives to avoid fallacies that can lead to self-deception."
—Professor Matthew Bennett, *Beyond the Supernatural: A Guide to Scientific Skepticism*

TOM PEERED AT HIS reflection in the elevator's mirrored walls. He noticed some stubble, but not enough to go back to his room and shave. *Relax. You're among friends.*

Tom took a few breaths as the elevator stopped on the main floor. The door slid open and a sign in the lobby caught his attention.

The Rosemont Desert Sun Hotel and Casino welcomes Habencon Attendees!

The sign prominently featured the logo of the Habenstein Society, founded by famous magician, infamous debunker, and father of the modern skeptical movement Reese Habenstein. Tom smiled as he left the elevator, knowing he was going to see his longtime role model and grandfather figure again.

Watching Reese's DVD as a child had changed Tom's life. After that night, he'd stopped reading the *Babbler* and started reading about science. Over the years, Tom and his father had bonded over skepticism, though growing up an unbeliever in Bolingbrook hadn't been easy.

Local youth groups were either religious or sponsored by churches. One time, an adult leader had warned Tom's parents he was an "at-risk youth" because he didn't go to church. He did go to Ethical Sunday School, but that was in the northern suburbs of Chicagoland, too far away to meet up more than once a week. Aging out hadn't helped matters either. In school, many kids had teased Tom, who became quiet and defensive around new people.

Being a shy teenager hadn't made dating easy. Hardly anyone wanted a hellbound boyfriend, and the young women he did date never became girlfriends. There were times when Tom considered pretending to be religious, but he always remembered Reese's commitment to the truth. Tom wasn't going to sacrifice who he was to seem cool.

Jason had tried to help by taking him to the Chicago Anti-Superstition Society's Saturday sessions. Though most attendees were older, Tom loved the sense of belonging he felt, and even developed a crush on one of the regulars, never finding the courage to tell her. After she found a boyfriend in college, Tom had been too sad to attend meetings.

College had been somewhat better, and Tom had managed to let his guard down and make more friends. Though he never entered a long term relationship, he dated, and even had his first sexual experience. They soon broke up, and though Tom kept asking women on dates, some of the breakups had been too painful to bounce back from. Plus, even in college, some women didn't like that he was an atheist who got carried away ranting against bunk.

Tom navigated through the maze of slots and video poker machines towards the familiar Old West facade of the Watering Hole bar. Looking at the signs with fake bullet holes excited him. This would be his third year at Habencon, Reese's annual convention of skeptics from around the world. Celebrities, scientists, teachers, and grassroots activists made the pilgrimage to Rosemont for a weekend of workshops, speeches, entertainment, and networking; and, of course, to honor the man who brought them together. At his previous Habencons, Tom had felt like he was surrounded by a group of special friends, and couldn't wait to experience it again.

Traditionally, attendees who arrived the day before Habencon gathered at the Watering Hole. Tom entered and quickly realized he'd never seen it this crowded before. The bar would have resembled a Wild West saloon, except for the big screen TVs hanging on wireframes. The staff uniforms resembled nineteenth century outfits, though

Tom doubted any waitress from that era would have worn a leotard and fishnet stockings.

Tom saw many familiar faces, but also that the Watering Hole gathering was less informal than it used to be. Vendors, organizations, podcasters, and bloggers now reserved tables where their fans could congregate and buy merchandise. Two of them captured his interest. The *Skeptical World* podcasters had two tables loaded with books, CDs, and DVDs for sale. *SW*, Tom remembered, was one of the first podcasts about scientific skepticism and still the most popular. As he made his way towards the tables, he remembered when his father heard him listening to *SW*. "It's like a radio show for skeptics," his father had told him. Tom suspected that his father had been happy his teenage son was still interested in skepticism.

Next to *SW* was *SheSkeptic*, a skeptical women's blog. The people gathered by their table, however, were more interested in watching an interview being recorded, possibly for *Skeptical World*. Tom recognized the interviewer as Jamie Kyle, co-host of *SW* and editor of *SheSkeptic*. The ends of her medium-length blonde hair were neon pink, and she wore a pair of wire-rimmed glasses. Three women sat at the table with her, while three more stood behind.

"Something needed to be done about the lack of women here," said Jamie. "So we started the *SheSkeptic* scholarships. Let's meet the first recipients." Jamie pointed her microphone at the woman sitting to her right.

"I'm Pamela Gorman," the woman replied. She sported a blonde pixie cut and wore a purple t-shirt with a black cat on the front. "I'm a mathematics-physics graduate from Reed, where I also dabbled a bit in gender studies and music. This fall, I'm starting grad school at the University of Washington."

Jamie nodded. "Impressive. Now—is Sakura here?" As she glanced in Tom's direction, he quickly looked away, continuing towards the book tables.

At the *SW* table, he recognized three other hosts, two from Australia, and one, Ivan Cabot, from the US. While the Australians dressed casually, Ivan wore a t-shirt from the previous Habencon covered with pro-skepticism buttons. Tom wondered if Ivan was trying to compensate for being the newest and youngest member of *SW's* team.

Ivan noticed Tom. "Excuse me," he said. "Have we met before?"

Tom smiled. The thrill of being recognized never got old. "Last year. I'm Tom Larsen. I write the *Skeptical Butterfly* blog."

"That's right! You're that Tom. Good to see you again."

"Same here." They shook hands.

"You're from Bolingbrook, right?"

Tom felt his face burn red. "Guilty. In fact, I'm going to start working there in a few months."

"Not at the *Babbler*, I hope?"

Tom laughed. "Of course not. They'd fire me in an instant! I'm gonna debunk them."

"Good. We need to take the fight to their turf."

Tom nervously chuckled. "I will, but I'd rather focus on homeopathy. I know too many people who think that stuff works."

"I feel you," nodded Ivan, who then reached for a book. "We just got the new *Teen Guide to Skepticism*."

Tom felt the nostalgia rush over him. As a teenager, he'd won arguments because of that book. Still, that was the past, and he didn't need such a basic guide any more. "I'll think about it."

Tom looked at the other items on the table. Two CDs caught his attention. The first was Jamie's newest musical album, *Far Away*, its cover photoshopped to seem as if she was wearing a stretch of outer space. The second was by the host of the *Skeptical Minute* podcast, who wore a black tuxedo and held out his hand. A photoshopped lens flare floated above his open palm. Kneeling beside him was a naked woman, who was reaching towards the light while averting her eyes.

"In case you're wondering," Ivan said. "That's his wife." He grinned. "Lucky guy."

Tom let his eyes linger on her for a moment, then chuckled nervously. "I guess."

"Great skeptic too. His rapping, however..."

Tom shrugged, then paid for both albums.

"Thanks," Ivan said as he returned Tom's card. "Your purchases help keep us going."

"Glad to help," Tom replied. He took a few seconds to work up his courage. "You know," he finally said. "I've wanted to interview you since you joined the show."

"And I've been meaning to ask you."

Tom gasped.

"Yeah. I might not have recognized your face at first, but I've heard a lot about you. I think our audience would love to learn more about the blogger behind *Skeptical Butterfly*."

"Wow," Tom replied.

"If you keep up the work," Ivan added, "you'll have opportunities in the movement that you've never imagined."

"Wow." Tom collected himself. "I hope so. Podcasters' Row?"

"Where else? Stop by whenever."

Tom's face glowed with excitement as he left. Ivan would be the most famous person he'd ever interviewed. More importantly, Ivan wanted to interview him.

Tom shifted over to the Committee for Humanism and Skepticism's table. The Committee was one of the oldest international humanist organizations, founded by former CEO turned philosopher Paul Randall. Reese had run the Committee's skepticism branch until he left to form the Habenstein Society. At the Committee's peak, it had chapters on every continent but Africa, and was the largest atheist organization in the world. Though it was less popular now, rich donors and an international staff of activists kept it relevant.

Since the Committee catered mostly to its big donors, it didn't surprise Tom that they were promoting a cruise ship tour with Randall and Barqah Jogi, a committee member best known for critiquing Islam. As much as Tom wanted to hear her lectures, the cheapest room cost more than his expected salary. The staffers at the table showed little interest in him, so he looked around for his friends instead.

Moments later, he noticed a man wearing a familiar sports jacket. Tom realized he was standing a few feet away from skepticism's most influential intellectual and, arguably, the man responsible for the rise of atheism in the twenty-first century, Professor Matthew Bennett. Even Tom's religious friends knew who Bennett was and hated him. Since the publication of *The Skeptical Mind*, his books were bestsellers no matter the topic. Any of his controversial tweets could generate editorials around the world. Right now, Bennett was watching a tired-looking woman leave his table.

Tom took a deep breath, then approached. Though Bennett was in his late fifties, Tom couldn't see a single gray hair. Bennett's attention lingered for a few seconds on his departing companion, then turned to Tom.

"I hope this isn't a bad time," Tom blurted out.

Bennett shook his head. "I'll find her later. What can I do for you?"

"Um." Tom stuttered. "I'm Tom, and I just wanted to say I'm a big fan."

"Thank you." Bennett motioned for Tom to have a seat.

Tom rushed to take it, not knowing how much time he'd get with Bennett. "I especially enjoyed your debate with that postmodernist. I can't believe there are people like that."

"They're out there, that's for sure. They just have to learn that because some people are sexist, that doesn't mean the speed of light is a social construct. Amazing we debate that at all."

"I know. Well, thank you for standing up to them."

"You're welcome," Bennett replied. "So, what are your plans for this weekend? Any dates lined up?"

"Dates?"

"Hookups, dates, whatever you want to call them. I expect to do well this year. How about you?"

Tom blushed.

"You can trust me," Bennett said with a smile. "I used to be licensed." He paused as Tom tilted his head. "Wasn't worth it."

Tom nervously laughed.

"So. Dates?"

Tom looked around. He lowered his voice and leaned closer to Bennett. "Well, I don't like saying 'hookup.' It just sounds like you're using someone."

Bennett barely shrugged.

"I think of it as... making a connection."

"I'm interested."

"It's like... when most of us come here, we feel like we're part of something greater. Like it's us against the world, except here they can't reach us. My first time here, I took a chance and flirted with another scholarship recipient. She flirted back. It was amazing." He smiled as he reminisced.

"Who?"

"You wouldn't know her," Tom replied, believing she wouldn't have wanted him to say her name. "I've felt that way with other women I've met here." Tom nervously smiled. "It's something that doesn't happen to me outside—" Tom lowered his head. "Sorry. I must be boring you."

"Not at all."

"It's just so different at Habencon."

"It is. If I can ask, have you 'connected' with anyone famous?"

Tom shook his head. "I wouldn't have anything to say to them."

"You're a student, right?"

"I graduated."

"Congratulations. Welcome to the real world."

Tom chuckled. "Thanks."

"So that's something you can talk about."

"I don't know if—"

"Don't be modest. It won't get you far. In fact, if you want to get ahead, consider connecting with someone higher up."

Tom's eyes widened, surprised that someone like Bennett would say something like that.

Bennett continued, "You understand the importance of networking, right?"

Tom nodded.

"Horizontal networking is the best kind. Trust me." Bennett leaned closer. "I used to get paid a hundred bucks an hour to give advice. But I'll give you this one for free."

Tom nodded again and leaned closer to Bennett.

"Don't limit yourself," said Bennett. "You can have any woman you want."

Tom furrowed his brow. "Any?"

"Any," Bennett replied. "Just project confidence and make your move. Don't let anyone tell you differently. Worked for all my clients."

"That's it?" asked Tom.

"If you just want to"—Bennett paused—"*connect*, then yes. If you want something more... that's only the first step."

"There's more?"

"Yes," said Bennett, looking around the room, "But that's for another time." He stood, and Tom quickly stood up as well. "Remember, no one is out of your league. Only you can hold yourself back. Remember that."

"I will," Tom replied.

"I didn't catch your last name."

"Larsen."

"Tom Larsen?"

"Yes."

Bennett seemed to examine Tom for a moment. "Have fun, Tom. And remember, don't limit yourself."

"Thank you." Tom reached for his wallet.

"You can give me your card later. See you around, Tom." Bennett turned and faded into the crowd.

After a few moments, Tom realized his heart was racing. He took a few breaths to calm himself. Professor Matthew

Bennett not only talked to him but offered him free advice. It was a moment he never dreamed could happen.

A man's clapping startled Tom, who turned and saw an attendee with a mustache and a Habencon 2002 shirt rising from his chair. The other attendees fell silent, and many started looking in the same direction. At the entrance, Tom saw a familiar tall man with a muscular build, wearing a white-collared shirt and high-waisted pants that barely reached his shoes. His now-thinning, snowy white hair matched his trademark thick beard. It was the man who changed Tom's life, and who had changed the lives of many of the attendees. Reese Habenstein, magician, entertainer, debunker, and founder of the skeptical movement.

Most of the bar patrons took to their feet. Tom quickly started clapping, and soon the entire bar was giving Reese a standing ovation so loud Tom couldn't hear the slot machines outside. This was the third standing ovation Tom had seen at the bar, and each time, Reese seemed overwhelmed at the love directed at him. Eventually, the applause stopped, and the patrons started approaching him. Tom raced to the rapidly forming line.

Tom fondly remembered his first meeting with Reese and how friendly he was. It also surprised him when he started receiving occasional personal emails from Reese; but Tom always enjoyed their face to face conversations at Habencon much more, even if they were way too short.

Tom joined the line and then noticed Pamela standing behind him.

"Excuse me," asked Tom. "You're one of the *SheSkeptic* scholars, right?"

She nodded. "I'm Pamela."

"Right. Pamela..." Tom looked for her badge, then remembered registration started tomorrow morning.

"Gorman."

"Gorman. Now I remember. Tom Larsen."

"Pleased to meet you. Is this your first one too?"

Tom shook his head. "Third."

"Wow."

Tom felt confidence growing within him. "I've been a skeptic since I was a kid."

"Really?"

Tom closed his eyes for a few seconds, then recited Bennett's definition of scientific skepticism from memory.

A man behind Pamela clapped, and Tom did a quick bow.

"Wow," Pamela replied. "You really have it down."

"It's one of my favorite lines from *The Skeptical Mind*."

"I'll have to check it out."

"You should," Tom replied. "It's required reading for all skeptics."

The line inched closer towards Reese.

Tom continued. "So, why did you decide to come?"

"I recently started reading *SheSkeptic*, and when I read about the science workshops at Habencon, I had to come. Hopefully, they'll help me do effective public outreach to combat innumeracy. I mean, just look at them." She gestured at the people playing the slot machines. "That's innumeracy in action."

Tom glanced at the back doors. When he looked forward, he realized to his surprise that he was next in line.

Reese looked down and smiled as Tom approached. "Hi," he exclaimed. "I'm glad you came back!"

"You know I couldn't miss it."

The two shook hands.

"Dad says hi. He's sorry he couldn't make it this year."

"Too bad. I'm sure the new repair shop takes up all of his time."

"It does."

"So, how about you?"

"I'm now officially a college graduate."

Reese patted Tom on the arm. "I remember. You're going to be working for a newspaper, right?"

Tom grinned. "I start at the *Bolingbrook Star* next month. I'm going to be the Assistant Editor."

"Editor? Congratulations."

"Thanks, but it's really a reporter position."

"Don't apologize. Do you know how many journalism graduates never get to use their degrees?"

"I see your point."

"Good. So, are you going to take on the *Babbler*?"

"Absolutely! Though, really, I'll probably focus more on alt-med frauds. No one believes the *Babbler*."

"True. Still, the *Babbler's* been a pain in my ass for years."

Tom noticed impatient people pooling up behind him. "Before I go," Tom said. "Let me introduce you to Pamela. This is her first Habencon."

"A first timer," said Reese as his face lit up. "You're one of Jamie's scholarship winners. Welcome. Are you excited?"

As Reese and Pamela began talking, Tom walked to the bar and ordered a drink. As he sipped it, he noticed a few of his usual friends nearby. He tried to decide who to approach first.

"Tom?" Tom turned and saw Pamela approaching him "I have a meeting with the other scholarship recipients, but I should be back later tonight."

"I'll be around." Tom replied.

"Great. Oh—this might be a silly question, but do you blog?"

Tom reached for his wallet. "Of course. Mine's called *Skeptical Butterfly*." He handed her a card.

"I'll have to check it out."

"I like to think my little blog can make a big difference someday. Just like the wings of a butterfly can cause a hurricane."

"Not really." Pamela winked. "Nice sentiment, though."

"Thanks," Tom said with a smile.

***

Even after all the drinks, Tom felt lucky to be at a table with
Matthew and Reese, with Pamela alongside him. At the
far end, a reporter from the *Rosemont Star* sat with some
people he didn't know. Tom wasn't sure exactly when he'd
joined them, but now it was close to 2 AM.

"I've charted it out," Bennett interrupted. "The posi-
tives of pleasure are greater than the supposed negatives of
lacking full consent."

"You charted it out?" Pamela asked.

"Yes," Bennett continued. "Charting morality scientifi-
cally is an important new tool and the subject of my next
book."

Pamela tilted her head. "I don't think you can chart
something like that, and I say that as a mathematician."

"My research will—"

Reese started laughing, and the table fell silent. He set
down his plastic cup filled with clear soda. "You know,
something funny always happens when someone gets a
PhD. They spend years studying, theorizing, and defending their work. Finally, they produce a dissertation. If it
passes the committee, it's over. They've furthered humanity's understanding of the world. Then after all that intellectual work"—he paused—"their brain shuts down."

Bennett began to speak, but Reese held his forefinger
up. "Yet each one of them still feels the need to offer an
opinion on any subject, no matter how little they really know." Bennett's eyes narrowed, but Reese continued.
"So, let's stick to debunking the supernatural and alternative medicine here, shall we?"

Bennett started to reply, but stopped as Jamie approached.

"Hey," she told Reese. "Thanks for the magic lesson. Hopefully, I'll still remember most of it after this weekend."

Reese shrugged. "If you forget, just let me know. I'll review it for you."

"Sure," Jamie replied. She turned her attention to the rest of the table. "It's been a long night, and I need to go to bed."

"Too bad," Bennett said. "We were just talking about sex and feminism. I'd love to hear your thoughts on the subject."

Jamie shrugged. "I don't really consider myself a feminist, but as long as both people agree, they can do whatever they want." Jamie waved to everyone at the table. "Night, everyone. I signed up for way too much this weekend and I gotta crash now."

As Jamie left, Tom remembered Bennett's advice. Tom had been a fan of Jamie's for years. Her humor livened up the US portion of *Skeptical World,* and her artistic sensibilities balanced the strict scientific views of her fellow podcasters. Her songs varied from whimsical musings on astronomical units, to angry denouncements of religion, to uplifting affirmations of living a secular life, to somber reflections on facing life's hardships without a god. As Jamie walked towards the door, Tom stood up.

"I should get to bed too," he said. "It's been fun."

Once the others had said goodbye, Tom started towards the elevators. To his relief, he felt tipsy, but otherwise fine.

"Excuse me?"

Tom turned to find Pamela catching up with him.

"I just wanted to say I enjoyed chatting tonight. Maybe we can get together again? I'd like to hear more about the Ethical Union."

"Sure," Tom replied. "Shoot me an e-mail or send me a text. I know an excellent restaurant here that's actually affordable."

"Great!" Pamela said with a smile. "I'll let you get to bed."

"Good night."

Tom turned and hurried through the maze of slot machines. To his surprise, he saw Jamie still standing in the elevator bay. Tom smiled and approached. The door opened and Jamie, who hadn't noticed him, entered the elevator. Tom followed.

Chapter 2

"It was 2 AM and I announced I had to go to bed. After I left the bar, this guy followed me into the elevator. It was just him and me. On the way up, he said he was a huge fan and wanted me to come to his room. To all my male fans out there: Don't be that guy."
—Jamie Kyle, "Habencon 9 Wrap Up"

"Jamie wants to be raped. Someone should give her what she wants."
—@Skownway88

TOM PRESSED RECORD, HOPING this would be his last take.

"Three years. Three years of needless division, undermining the fight against superstition and the defense of science.

"The damage is clear. Declining attendance at Haben-con. Slanderous hearsay against members of the Committee for Humanism and Skepticism. Demands for over-bearing rules at gatherings and ideological purity. While society has kept evolving, feminism is devolving.

"The truth is, both men and women made the skeptical movement what it is. They stood up against marketers who exploit women. They denounce sexist theocracies across the world. They fight against fundamentalists who want to tear down separation of church and state. The skeptical movement fights for women in the face of unrelenting attacks.

"In three years, what have feminists done for skepticism? They started a forum called Humanist Heart. They're trying to replace the Committee and the Habenstein Society. They were going to gather in Rosemont for a so-called congress but bailed. So, in three years, all they have to show for their work is an echo chamber, a failed convention, and a divided movement.

"I should also mention this conflict is harming families. Here's an email I received. 'Dear Tom. My brother is like you. He doesn't believe in God and girls bully him. It makes him mad. He yells at Mom and me. I know you can help. Meggy, your biggest fan.'

"What a sad story. Hang in there, Meggy.

"Emails like this are why I maintain *Skeptical Hurricane*. You can help me by liking this video and subscribing to my channel. You can also make a one-time donation, or become a member of the Skeptical Hurricane Network. I want to thank all my members for their support."

Tom shut off the camera and added the clip to the rest of his video. After uploading it, he stood and stretched. Tom happily pictured his viewers on his way to the kitchen, where the smell of burning chicken greeted him. *Fuck.*

Three years ago, Jamie Kyle had turned a short conversation into an Internet scandal. Tom had read and heard comments about "Elevator Guy," but assumed it would all blow over. A week later, however, the *Bolingbrook Star* had rescinded his job offer. They never offered an explanation, but Tom knew why.

Tom grabbed a grubby oven mitt and pulled two dry chicken breasts from the grill, casually plating his dinner.

After losing the job, he had asked Reese if he could work for him. Reese said he would give him a chance once things had settled down, and promised Tom that if he didn't disclose his role in "the incident," he would have access to a "very important level in the movement."

Tom had kept his promise to Reese, but that hadn't stopped him from criticizing feminists. It felt good to vent his anger at Jamie and her allies. At first, he'd limited himself to blogging in case Jamie saw his face. To his surprise, traffic to his blog grew. His new readers didn't understand why Jamie and other female skeptics were suddenly so critical towards prominent men.

Then the donations started coming in. First, it was through his PayPal page—so much money, in fact, that PayPal started asking questions. Once Tom had set up crowdfunding pages, the money coming in stunned him. Within six months, he quit working for his dad, moved into his own apartment, and started working full time creating online content. Tom later added a podcast and YouTube channel, creating a network of content. He worried Jamie might recognize him, but if she did, she never publicly mentioned it. He suspected she'd moved on to complaining about other people criticizing her.

Reese had sent him an email claiming that his new content would "only make it harder to hire you." Then emails from him had dropped considerably. Reese's last email, sent a few months ago, said he was on the verge of fixing things, whatever that meant.

Tom found himself at the kitchen table, about to squirt a bottleful of BBQ sauce onto the chicken. An open Mountain Dew was next to him. Tom didn't remember sitting down or opening it.

Tom felt a buzz in his pocket, pulling out his phone and seeing an email from Isaac, a fan and source in one of the major skeptical orgs. He suspected it was the Habenstein Society, but all he really knew was that all Isaac's leads were accurate. He also offered great blogging advice.

> Not a bad video. The let-
> ter was a pleasant touch.
> But you went too easy
> on Humanist Heart. Don't
> assume it's over because
> they lost the Desert Sun.
> They still have time to
> book a new venue. I'm copy-

> *ing in Marty Nowak and*
> *Trevor DeBruin. Marty is*
> *coordinating the protests*
> *in Chicagoland. He also*
> *lives in Bolingbrook. You*
> *know who Trevor is.*

Tom didn't know who Marty was, but Trevor was one of his favorite gender equality vloggers. Whenever anyone argued that all critics of feminism were raging misogynists, all someone had to do was show one of his videos. Trevor's clean appearance, well-reasoned videos, and politeness would silence them. His demeanor earned him high praise from some leading skeptics. Matthew Bennett even called him a modern-day Susan B. Anthony. Tom didn't agree with Trevor on everything, but he did listen to him, which was more than most feminists did.

Tom resumed reading.

> *The most important—*

The screen turned black as his cell phone started ringing. Tom swore and wondered why his dad always called and never texted.

"Hi, Dad."

Jason hesitated. Tom suspected it was because he still wasn't used to others having caller ID. "Have I caught you at a bad time?"

"Not really."

"Just wanted you to know we won an award for having one of the best kept lawns in Bolingbrook."

"Congratulations. I guess?"

"We want you to join us tomorrow when we get the plaque from Robert."

"Robert?"

"Mayor Robert Clark. He's handing out the plaques."

"Oh, that guy. Um. Sounds great, but I have plans."

"Tom, this is really important. Especially for your mother."

Tom sighed. "I guess I can go."

"Thank you. Oh, I have some good news."

"Good news?"

"The Chicago Anti-Superstition Society will be hiring soon."

"Dad! I'm already self-employed."

"I see. I guess."

"What is it, Dad?"

Jason paused for a few moments. "I know you're making money off the blog—"

"You mean my network."

His father paused again. "Tom, your mother and I worry about you."

Tom sighed.

"We do," his father continued. "You hardly visit us. When you do, you hardly say anything. Have you seen any of your old friends? Are you seeing anyone?"

"No, and no. I'm especially not seeing anyone."

"A man your age—"

"Some men my age are going their own way. Modern feminists are ruining dating, Dad. They're even restricting where you can and can't talk to a woman. When things calm down, I'll jump back in."

"We're not just worried about that. You used to love being involved in the movement. You said you wanted to be a professional skeptic when you grew up."

"I am."

"No, you make money *off* skepticism. If you want to impact the movement, work within an organization."

"That's so dated," Tom replied.

"It's not," Jason countered. "You'd have more influence and resources if you worked with one of the major groups. Your blogging could help you negotiate a salary. Have you even followed up on any of the leads I've given you?"

Tom sighed.

Jason continued. "The Committee is still looking for people. I don't know how Paul's still holding it together, but you could help him."

"I suppose. But honestly, I don't want to work for a man who tried to replace the Humanist Manifestos with his own creed. He's brilliant, but so full of himself."

"Okay," Jason replied. "How about CAS? They've stayed out of the rift and do great work. They're well-funded, and I know you would get a decent salary."

Tom shook his head. "I know they have big donors."

"Their leadership is fairly young for a skeptical organization. The president might remember you. She was a regular when we used to go to their lunch lectures."

Tom sighed and closed his eyes.

"What's wrong?" Jason asked.

Tom fought the urge to hang up. "It's complicated."

"I have time," Jason replied. "Explain to me why you don't want to work for CAS. I know you had your heart broken back then, but that was years ago."

Tom cringed. "Dad—"

"Forget I mentioned her. Tom, I'm worried about you. I can read between the lines. You're trying to come across as reasonable, but I know something's upsetting you."

"I'm upset that feminists are ruining the movement and trying to ruin society."

After a few moments, Jason replied, "You know, your mother considers herself a feminist."

"I know she's a feminist. I'm not writing about her. I'm writing about modern feminists. That's what the movement needs to focus on. Bigfoot and aliens can wait."

"What about anti-vaxxers?"

"Fine, we can focus on them as well. But you know what I'm talking about, right? We have to fight back against their baseless accusations. You know what they're saying about Bennett."

Jason paused. "We can talk about it later."

"Fine," Tom snapped.

"We'd like to pick you up tomorrow and have you at the ceremony. Like I said, it would mean a lot to your mother."

"Sure," Tom replied.

"And please don't talk about what you're doing online. Your mother won't understand."

"I won't."

"You know, maybe it would have been better if we'd raised you in Evanston or Skokie. We'd have been closer to the Society, and you'd have been around more kids like you."

"We'll never know," Tom said. He ended the call before his father replied.

Tom set down his phone as he remembered the times in his childhood when he felt isolated. As he aggressively sliced up what remained of the chicken breast, he pondered what he could have changed; what he should have done; all the missed chances.

Tom's phone alarm snapped him back to reality. Almost time for a group call. After snoozing it, he rushed to finish his meal, then added his dishes to the pile in the sink.

***

After a ten-minute car ride during which his parents argued about who ruined alternative music—Alanis Morissette or Stained—Tom found himself at Town Center, Bolingbrook's equivalent to a village hall. On stepping inside the boardroom, he wondered if he'd wandered into a TV studio by mistake. Instead of the cramped, windowless room he'd expected, the boardroom had a row of two-story windows along the right-hand side. Outside, Tom could see the US, Illinois, and Bolingbrook flags fluttering in the summer breeze.

There were two elevated platforms along the back wall. The village trustees sat on the highest level with the other officials on the lower one. Tom noticed automated cameras on the ceiling and in the corners of the boardroom, while ahead there were rows and rows of movie theater chairs for the audience. Between them and the platform was an open area, furnished with a table of plaques and a microphone stand. Jason and Tom sat down on the cushioned theater style seats.

As Michelle was about to sit, Mayor Robert Clark casually strolled into the room. Tom thought the mayor had changed little since their first meeting years ago. From where he sat, Robert still towered over him, though unlike their last meeting, he now had a full head of gray hair.

Tom watched as Robert talked to a family sitting at the front. Michelle approached. Tom couldn't hear what they were saying, but both were motioning towards the awards table.

Jason shook his head.

"Dad?"

"Tom, I think your mother will want a picture of us with Robert."

Tom shrugged. "Okay."

Michelle returned and sat next to Jason. Robert took the microphone from its stand and called the meeting to order. The audience, except for a few toddlers, fell silent.

A local veteran recited the Pledge of Allegiance. Robert, acting like a seasoned award show host, started calling up individual families to receive their Bolingbrook Beautification plaques. Robert called out to the Miller family, then stepped up to escort the parents and their young daughter to the table.

"I should point out that the Miller family represents three generations of Bolingbrook residents," said Robert. "In fact, Blake, your father was the first person who welcomed me to Bolingbrook. So, I'm honored to give this award to your family."

"Um, we just hire a lawn care—"

"We appreciate it. It may not seem like much, but the work you've done keeps our suburb attractive. It's one reason Bolingbrook is among the fastest-growing communities in Illinois."

"Okay. Um, thanks."

"No—thank you." Robert smiled, then looked down at their daughter. "You must be Jenny."

She nodded.

"How old are you?" He lowered the mic for her.

"Four."

"That's a great age. What do you want to be when you grow up?"

"I wanna be mayor!"

Robert turned and mugged at the audience as they laughed. He turned back to Jenny. "I'm sure you will. Just don't run against me!"

"Okay!"

Robert presented the Millers with their plaque. After posing for pictures, he directed them back to their seats.

Robert then called up Jason and Michelle. As they moved forward, Tom positioned himself next to two photographers, and started taking pictures with his smartphone.

Robert acknowledged Tom's parents, then faced the audience. "Now, I remember when the Larsens moved to Bolingbrook." He dramatically put his left hand above his eyes and scanned the audience. "Is your son here?"

Tom held up his hand.

Robert pulled his head back. Tom couldn't tell if he was acting or genuinely surprised. "I hardly recognize you."

"It has been a while," Tom shrugged. Robert pivoted back to Jason and Michelle.

"Jason, why don't you tell us about your business?"

Jason gave what Tom recognized as his elevator pitch for the repair shop. Robert nodded and praised him for creating local jobs.

"So, Michelle? Tell us about yourself."

"I volunteer at the library, and our family is active in the Northern Chicago Ethical Union, which is founded on the belief the best values come not from a higher power but from living a life grounded in reason and guided by the heart."

Tom heard some muttering behind him. Robert looked towards the audience and held up his hand. The muttering ended. He turned back towards Tom's parents.

"I actually know a few people who share your beliefs. They do important work."

Michelle smiled and nodded. Jason accepted the plaque from Robert and walked back to his seat. Michelle thanked Robert, then followed him back.

Robert handed out several more awards. After presenting the last, he called for a short recess. Jason and Tom stood up as the families left.

"That was okay," said Tom. "And I'll be able to make my group call tonight."

"Actually," said Michelle, still sitting, "I think we should stay and watch the rest."

Jason stopped walking. Tom almost lost his balance as he stopped next to him.

"You're serious about this?"

"Yes."

"About what?" asked Tom.

"I think I should run for the Fountaindale Library Board. Julie is retiring, and I like the other board members. I think I'd be a great fit."

Tom swallowed. "You know—"

"I think it's a great idea," Jason interrupted. "You need to see Robert's political machine in action before becoming a cog."

Tom locked over at Robert, who was talking to someone, and probably didn't hear Jason over the crowd. Tom looked down at his phone. He'd never make his meeting if they stayed.

"Dad—"

"You live in Bolingbrook. You need to see what your mother wants to join."

"You don't have to phrase it that way," Michelle replied.

"Fine," Jason said. "Just watch the meeting, then. If you still want to run, I won't try to stop you."

Tom sighed and sat back down next to his dad. His family, and a few others, were the only ones left in the audience.

Robert called the meeting back to order, the other officials snapping to attention as he rapped the gavel. After approving the minutes, the racially diverse trustees unanimously passed the first three funding resolutions without debate.

"There hasn't been a 'no' vote cast since 2010," Jason whispered. "Everyone up there is a member of Robert's party. The person who voted no? Gone."

"Maybe Robert is just good at his job," countered Michelle.

After three more unanimous yes votes, the clerk read a resolution authorizing a transfer of funds to the Bolingbrook Golf Club. Tom remembered reading the *Babbler's* fantastic claims about the club. After the reading, Robert spoke.

"I recently spoke with representatives of a group that had their convention canceled because of threats. I offered them the Bolingbrook Golf Club's facilities, and they agreed. These funds will improve our security, which will benefit both this convention and future gatherings. If we can show our Golf Club is one of the most secure facilities in Illinois, more bookings will follow."

"Good luck," Jason whispered. "The club is on the edge of nowhere. You might as well hold a convention in the desert."

"I heard it's a very nice club," Michelle whispered back. "We've always wanted to go there for the Fourth of July."

Jason shook his head.

"What is the name of this organization?" asked a trustee Tom didn't recognize.

"Humanist Heart International. They're a new social justice group. Their convention is in three weeks. Again, this is an opportunity to promote the Golf Club as a secure facility. I don't necessarily agree with their views."

"Still," the trustee replied. "Didn't they find a bomb at their previous hotel?"

"They did. I feel, however, that the Golf Club is unbreachable."

The resolution passed. Several minutes later, Robert opened the floor to questions from the media. A man wearing a patched-up sports coat walked up to the podium.

"Make it quick."

"I will, Robert. Many residents of Bolingbrook report memory gaps. Are these the result of illegal extraterrestrial probes?"

There was a long pause as the trustees turned to Robert.

"Don," Robert finally replied. "I heard you're retiring this week."

"Yes, I am. I've been writing for the *Babbler* since 1983."

"I hope you're irreplaceable," Robert replied. A few of the trustees chuckled. "That's my quote for today. Goodbye."

Don nodded and stepped away from the podium. He looked at the front row where two men in suits were sitting. "I won't miss you guys," muttered Don on his way out.

Tom noticed he'd been clenching his chair's armrests since first hearing Humanist Heart's name. The group that wanted to usurp the movement wasn't dead, and had found a site for its congress in his hometown with the blessing of the mayor. Tom suspected that Jamie Kyle was behind Humanist Heart, which meant she was coming to Bolingbrook. This wasn't a convention: this was an invasion. Tom released the armrests, then charged towards the podium, forcefully adjusting the microphone when he reached it.

"You don't need to pull so hard," said Robert.

"Sorry," said Tom.

"State your name and address. You have one minute." Robert looked down at his papers.

"Tom Larsen, Promenade View Apartments. I just want to say I'm angry that you're bringing Humanist Heart into our community."

Tom enjoyed the adrenaline rush from releasing his anger. He stopped holding it back.

"You are providing a platform for a feminist cult. They want to destroy science and reason and trade it for their ideology. I am here representing residents of Bolingbrook and rationalists who say enough. You will not intimidate us. Deal with your fear of elevators and leave Bolingbrook alone."

"I'm not afraid of elevators," said Robert, looking bemused.

"I was talking about—"

Robert shuffled his papers. "Sounds like you don't want to be there. Good news. You don't have to be."

"I'll be there. I'm a member of the media. Residents have the right—"

"Are you registered with the village clerk?"

"Registered?"

"Yes. We can't have just anyone with a blog claim they're a member of the media. That wouldn't be fair to the working press. We ask all media outlets to register with the village clerk's office. You can find her after this meeting."

A woman sitting on the lower level of the platform raised her hand.

Tom acknowledged her, then turned to Robert. "I'll register with her, but you have to—"

"Time," said Robert.

"What?"

Robert looked at Tom, his eyes sparkling. "Your time is up, Mr. Larsen. Goodbye."

Chapter 3

"The mission of skeptical organizations is to promote skepticism. Anything else is mission drift."
—@thativancabot

As Tom approached the strip malls along Barber's Corner in his blue Toyota Echo, he could make out the words *Bolingbrook Babbler* among the red brick buildings. The gray concrete slab roofs brought World War II bunkers to mind. Across Route 53, he could see the new Portillo's building and the businesses that replaced the East Boughton Drive Jewel-Osco store where his parents used to shop.

Tom made a left turn on the access road. After a short drive, he turned into the parking lot and soon found himself in front of the *Babbler's* office. Two days ago, he never would have imagined himself here.

After the board meeting, still high from his public comments, Tom had approached the village clerk, thinking she would give him a form to fill out to become a registered Bolingbrook media outlet. Instead, she recorded his information and said she had a backlog of applications to approve. Tom suspected she wasn't telling him the truth. She suggested Tom ask one of the registered outlets to sponsor him. Otherwise, he could be waiting at least a month.

The drive home had been one of the worst car trips he'd taken with his parents since they went to Malta, Illinois and got lost in the corn maze. This time his parents ceaselessly grilled him on his remarks. When they offered to pay for him to see a therapist, Tom refused. As his parents kept insisting he needed help, Tom wondered why his mother, whom he considered a rational feminist, didn't understand.

The next day had only made matters worse. He emailed all the suburban newspapers, asking if any were interested in a story about the Humanist Heart congress. As a joke, he even emailed a pitch to the *Babbler*, penning a fake story in their style. He remembered laughing as he emailed them. Surely, he thought, at least one serious news outlet would accept his pitch. How could they not cover a feminist invasion of suburbia?

None of the area papers were interested—one editor even offered to pray for him. Well, almost none. The editor of the *Babbler* had been interested, and insisted on meeting in person.

Tom stood at the front door. Painted on the glass were the words: *Bolingbrook's first and only true tabloid since 1965.* Tom let out a sigh and trudged in.

Entering a room of brown cubicles, Tom heard some members of staff talking on the phone, while others typed away at their keyboards. A front counter and two side counters separated the reception area from the newsroom. Framed copies of old *Babbler* issues lined the walls. To his far left, he saw a door and made out the word "Publisher." *Probably the only actual office in this building.*

Tom noticed a woman at an open-air desk. She was wearing a gray textured t-shirt and faded jeans. Tom thought she looked familiar, but couldn't recall why.

The woman looked up from her computer. "Can I help you?"

"I have a meeting with Sara," Tom replied.

"You must be Tom." She stood up and walked towards the counter. "I'm Wendy Onofrey. Pleased to meet you." Tom shook her hand. "Sara got called into a meeting with our publisher. Something about a job applicant." Wendy lifted the hinged part of the counter and opened a small door. "You can wait back here with me."

As Tom walked into the news area, Wendy motioned for him to sit in a chair by her desk.

"You wouldn't happen to be that job applicant?"

Tom shook his head. "Just submitting a piece. If it goes well, maybe she'll let me cover a special event at the Golf Club."

"Humanist Heart?"

Tom raised his eyebrows. "You've heard of them?"

"Of course," Wendy replied. "It's our job to know what's going on in Bolingbrook."

Tom fought the urge to make a snarky remark as he sat down. "I hope she'll let me cover it."

Wendy nodded. "If you do, investigate why they're holding it here. The Golf Club doesn't exactly scream social justice. Plus, Robert doesn't strike me as one of them. Though I think the official story is right about one thing: It would be the safest place. It is the secondary command center for Bolingbrook."

"Oh. I think I remember reading about that."

"A reader," Wendy replied. "I like that."

"Well—"

"Lots of residents just glance at our covers. I like the ones who take the time to read our articles."

Tom politely nodded, wondering when Sara's meeting would end.

Wendy continued. "Anyway. It'll be interesting to see what happens. Like I said, it's the safest place in Illinois, next to Clow Base, of course. Considering they found a bomb at the last location, they'll need the protection."

Tom chuckled. "I guess the village will protect them while they conspire against the skeptical movement."

Wendy shook her head. "Actually, that's not the point of this meeting. From what I've read, they're divided between the forum-only faction and the non-profit faction. So, this is really a congress about the future of the group. Do they stick with being an Internet space for progressive skeptics, or do they become a progressive version of the Habenstein Society? They also need to decide if they want to work with other groups. Since some of them will have observers there, it should be a lively event."

"I expect it will be. All the drama should interest your readers."

Wendy looked closer at Tom, then raised her finger. "Say, did you used to write a blog?"

"Still do. It's called *Skeptical Hurricane*."

"Oh." Wendy looked uncomfortable as she leaned away. "I remember when it was *Skeptical Butterfly*."

Tom failed to contain his surprise.

"Back when I posted on the Habenstein Society's forums," said Wendy, "I remember seeing a lot of links to your posts. I enjoyed reading them."

Tom furrowed his brow. "You used to be a skeptic?"

"Still am."

"You are?" Tom stumbled. "I didn't expect..."

"To find a skeptic here? Actually, this is the best place for a skeptic. I've learned more here than I ever did in the skeptical movement."

"You left the movement?"

"It left me."

"Onofrey? Are you related—"

"To the guy who trolls skeptics? Yes. We used to be identical."

"Oh," Tom replied.

The back door opened. A man and woman walked in, carrying bags and drinks from Portillo's.

"Lunchtime!" said the woman, who wore a black pantsuit and appeared to be close to Tom's age. Tom admired her copper hair for a moment, then turned his attention back to Wendy.

"Perfect," Wendy replied, then looked at Tom. "Portillo's day is one of the few perks we have."

Other staff members emerged from the cubicles. While the man placed most of the bags on a table, the woman approached with a bag marked for Wendy. Wendy accepted it, and the woman glanced at the publisher's office.

"They're still meeting?"

"Yep," Wendy replied. "I think he wasn't too pleased. Especially if he called Sara in."

The woman stared at the door for a few moments, then faced Wendy. "They should be done soon. Oh, your friend says thanks for lunch. He's seen two rifts this week."

"Thanks. I'll take care of it."

"Sure." The woman noticed Tom and stepped closer. "Have we met?"

"I don't think so."

"Excuse me," said Wendy. "I forgot my manners. Tom, this is Jenna Olson, our sales representative, and one of our resident psychics."

Jenna smiled. "Actually, I prefer the term percipient."

"Jenna," Wendy continued, "This is Tom. He wants to submit a piece."

"Oh!" said Jenna. "So, what's your article about?"

"You're asking?" said Tom.

"Yes?" Jenna replied.

"You're the psychic." Tom closed his eyes and imagined the answer. When he opened them, he saw Jenna frowning at him.

"That was rude," she said. "You shouldn't test someone without asking. And if you're going to, do the right test, because I have precognition, not telepathy."

"My apologies," Tom sarcastically replied. "I don't normally hang out with precogs."

"Don't mention that movie."

"Noted. So, what am I doing next week?"

Jenna glared at Tom for a moment, then her face relaxed. She tilted her head, then stepped closer, squinting her eyes for a few moments before straightening her posture and stepping back.

"That's odd," she said. "It seems like you're not doing anything next week."

"Nothing?"

"Nothing. Wait." She tilted her head again. "Something about you feels off."

"Off?" Tom asked. "Ah. I get it. You just need my credit card number to fine tune your vision."

"No," Jenna snapped.

"Something *is* wrong," added Wendy. "She should see something, even if you're dead next week."

"Yet I don't see or sense anything about you," said Jenna. "You're full of surprises, Tom."

"I suppose," Tom answered. "Or maybe you know better than to try a cold reading—"

"Really?" Jenna replied, frowning.

"She isn't a cold reader," said Wendy. "Notice she didn't flood you with questions."

"But she gave a vague answer."

"I was very specific," protested Jenna.

"'Nothing' is a specific answer?"

"Yes."

"So I'm going to cease to exist next week?"

Wendy shook her head. "More likely her brain can't process what she's seeing."

"Process?"

"Let me show you." Wendy picked up a business card and wrote Tom's name, placed the card in her hand, then turned both her palms down on the desk. "Where's the card?"

"Your other hand?"

Wendy showed Tom both of her empty palms. "Our brains make mistakes." She pulled the card out of her desk drawer and placed it in front of Tom. He saw his name written on it. "Our brains are evolved to make assumptions, and some of those assumptions are wrong—you were fooled by my misdirection. Jenna sees parts of the future, but can't always tell what she's looking at."

Tom reluctantly nodded.

"Reese taught me that trick," said Wendy. "If you want to be published in the *Babbler*, you really should be more open-minded."

Tom felt his face warm with embarrassment. He still didn't believe Jenna was a psychic, but he needed access to the congress.

"While I have questions," Tom sighed. "I'm sorry you were hurt by how I asked them."

"You're sorry I was offended?" asked Jenna.

"Yes," said Tom. He decided humor might lighten things. "I'm sorry, and I promise to never introduce you to Anti-Psychic Kitty."

"Tom," said Wendy. "Anti-Psychic Kitty almost killed her father."

"Seriously? The CAS's mascot? How?"

"That is a *very* long story," came a new voice. Tom turned and saw a Black woman in her late thirties wearing a white blouse with gray slacks. "Which my staff don't have time to tell because we have *an issue. To finish.*"

Tom stood up. "I'm—"

"I know who you are. Sara Langston, editor. We have a lot to talk about." She offered her hand, shaking Tom's firmly, then motioned for him to follow.

Jenna approached Tom. "Before you go, there's one thing I should tell you. Bolingbrook is known as the Pathway Village. Don't be afraid to change paths."

Jenna smiled before returning to Wendy's desk.

Tom gave Jenna a puzzled look, then followed Sara into her cubicle. The divider walls were bare, but behind the desk was a small bookshelf. On top of it were pictures he assumed were of her husband and daughter. Two books stood out to Tom: a worn copy of a guide to haunted places in Chicago, and one titled *Blood in the Wind: The Secret History of Chicagoland's Vampire Kingdoms and Free Territories.*

Sara motioned towards the chair in front of her desk. Tom sat and placed a printout of his article in front of her. For the first time since college, an editor was about to review his writing. Sara sat down, clicked her wireless mouse, and turned her attention to her screen. Tom removed a pen from his shirt pocket and set it next to the printout.

"You aren't making my job easy," said Sara.

"Oh?"

"Our publisher has concerns about printing anything by you. Insulting his granddaughter didn't help your case."

Tom suddenly felt like he'd swallowed a black hole. The Olson family owned the *Babbler*. He should have recognized Jenna's last name.

"Oh God," Tom heard himself whisper. "I can apologize right now. It's just—um. I'm sorry. It won't happen again."

"Good," Sara replied. "Considering Jenna's visions are one reason I invited you here, I hope you'll show her more respect."

"I will," Tom blurted out.

"That's good to hear. You can take a minute."

"Thank you," said Tom as he tried to calm himself down. After a few deep breaths, he relaxed. "I'm ready."

"Good. So, let's start with your sample story."

Tom felt his confidence return. "You're welcome to publish it, and if you need any minor corrections—"

"You made this up."

Tom waited several uncomfortable moments for Sara to continue. She continued to glare at him.

Say something.

"And?" asked Tom.

Sara leaned towards him. "You wrote a piece of fiction. A sloppy piece of fiction. We don't print fiction here."

Tom's jaw dropped. *How can I be blowing this?*

"Look at your story," said Sara. "It's about Gray-type aliens. There's no such thing as Grays. Then you brought Bigfoot into it. Bolingbrook doesn't have a Bigfoot population. Even if it did, aliens don't carry away Bigfoot corpses. They turn to dust. I also know you didn't interview any aliens. That's just the first paragraph." Tom gulped as Sara continued. "I could go on, but let me get to the point: We're not a literary magazine and we don't print fiction."

"Come on," Tom protested. "If I'm guilty of anything, it's not paying close attention to your recent stories. I'll read some more—"

"I said we don't publish fiction."

"But everyone in Bolingbrook knows your stories aren't real. *I* know they're not real. I grew up here. I've seen Hidden Lakes. I've walked the trails. We laugh at your articles because we know they're not real. You can't criticize me because my story is fiction when everything the *Babbler*'s ever published is fictional. And that's beside the point—I want to write about something real!"

Sara shook her head. "Maybe if I'd spent as many years among skeptics as you, I wouldn't think twice about submitting this. Maybe I'd feel like pranking the *Babbler* was serving humanity. But let me assure you, Tom. All the articles we publish are about something real."

Tom blinked. "Are you seriously trying to tell me you believe everything you publish?"

Sara leaned back in her chair and paused for a moment. "Of course I do. My name is on the masthead. Before I worked here, I thought the stories were fiction. But let's just say after I had a run-in with the men in blue, I became more open-minded. That nearly got me fired from my previous paper, but I wanted to know the truth. So, I feel very fortunate to work for the *Babbler*. Our content may seem like a joke to you, but we make sure we thoroughly research stories before publishing them. Do you believe me now?"

Tom considered the possibilities. "I... understand that you believe what you publish."

"That's a good start."

Time to recover.

"So, I apologize for writing a fiction piece. I didn't know how committed you and your staff are to reporting what you believe is the truth. I hope I can make up for it by writing a story—a real story—for you. Let me tell you what I have to offer."

"I'm listening," said Sara.

"Let's start with my YouTube channel."

"Let's not."

Tom swallowed.

Sara continued. "Let's talk about your blog. Back when it was *Skeptical Butterfly*, you did a good job. You were more thorough than most skeptics, even though you toed the party line. Then once your pass at Jamie Kyle backfired, you—"

"*You*!" Tom looked closer at Sara. His eyes widened. "You were at our table that night."

"I was. When I saw Jamie's video, it was obvious who she was talking about."

"You told my editor."

"Yes, but it wasn't my goal to get you fired. I wanted her to give you a warning. Our publisher, however, either feared a lawsuit or wanted an excuse to let you go. Were you aware of the layoffs that followed your release?"

Tom stood up and turned.

"I can get you into the Golf Club."

Tom stopped as desperation overpowered his anger. He turned and faced Sara, who was still sitting at her desk.

"I'm working on securing a press pass for the congress. If we don't get one, we have the connections necessary to get someone in undercover. Wendy has the background to cover the congress, but she's responsible for the layout and the website. I can't risk putting her out in the field."

"I see your point."

Sara continued. "I've looked at the stories you wrote in college. You were an excellent investigative journalist. That article on corruption in UIC's student government? Impressive."

"Thank you?" Tom replied, hesitant.

"Not every reporter can say they forced a politician to leave the country. You know where he is now?"

"I heard he's running a casino for the Russian mob."

"That's my understanding. It takes courage to do investigative journalism."

"I guess," Tom replied.

"But I have a question. Your blog says you're a man going your own way. Correct?"

"Basically."

"So why not keep going? You have a successful blog and podcast with thousands of followers. You're a leader in your movement, even if you don't think of yourself as one. Why do you have to go to this meeting? I won't send you there if you're just going to harass Jamie."

Tom's heart sped up again. "I'm not! This is—"

"Good. Sit down."

Tom sat down.

"What do you know about weredeer?"

***

Tom sighed as he drove east. It was after 11 PM, and to the north, he could just make out the old landfill mound—Mount Bolingbrook, as he liked to call it. To the south, he could see the fence securing the Elmhurst-Chicago quarry. *Another uneventful night.*

He'd read about weredeer in the *Babbler,* and unfortunately still remembered key details. They were like werewolves, except their animal phenotype was a deer. They could shift into one of three forms: humanoid, deer, and alpha. As Sara had reminded him, a weredeer in its alpha form could hold its own in a fight with a dire wolf. She had also reminded him they couldn't mate with each other. While they could mate with normal deer, some weredeer obsessively focused on mating with humans.

Sara had also claimed that there were two local factions of weredeer: suburban and feral. In the 1990s, the suburban weredeer, persuaded by the Bolingbrook Jaycees, agreed to abide by traditional human courtship customs, even if it reduced the chance of producing weredeer born from humans. In exchange, the village would recognize them as Bolingbrook residents. A minority rejected the deal. Not wanting to be hunted by the village's Department of Paranormal Affairs, the feral weredeer retreated to the forest preserves, pledging only to mate with deer.

As a teenager, Tom remembered laughing at the *Babbler's* blurry photos of weredeer in their alpha form. If anyone showed him a blurry photo of Bigfoot, Tom would counter by showing them a blurry photo of a weredeer. Why, Tom would ask, did people believe in Bigfoot but not weredeer, despite there being more photographic evidence for the latter? Some of his classmates told him he was an asshole, while others just called him Bolingbrook High's official class skeptic.

Now the class skeptic was driving down Royce Road trying to find a creature that only existed on the pages of the *Babbler*. According to Sara, hundreds of feral weredeer from around the country were gathering for unknown reasons in the nearby woods. His assignment was to investigate.

This was how Tom had spent most of the week. He'd interviewed all the people on Sara's list of weredeer eyewitnesses. Most sounded sincere, but no one had caught an unambiguous view of a weredeer. A few claimed to have seen something in the woods that moved too fast to be a normal deer. One witness said she'd been walking towards Hidden Lakes Historic Trout Farm and "heard a foreign-sounding voice." Then, she said, a deer had jumped out of the woods, and "glared" at her.

The field skepticism workshops at Habencon portrayed fieldwork as informative, exciting, and short. Old Man Jake from the Committee for Humanism and Skepticism had bragged about all the new skills he'd learned from his investigations, like how to break a board with his hands. The "ghost couple" from France had claimed they could debunk any haunted site in a single night. The Open Investigations Team had countless funny videos debunking psychics. Tom wasn't learning anything, he wasn't having fun, and wasn't even close to resolving the "weredeer mystery." Exhausted and frustrated, he took comfort in knowing that he only had one more area to check out before he could go to bed. Fortunately, it was close to his apartment.

From his phone, which was plugged into the Echo's stereo, Trevor DeBruin's voice jolted Tom back to the present. "It is time to put away the beliefs that now drive feminism," he said. "Time for a philosophy that celebrates sexuality instead of shaming men. Time for a society that does not favor females. If saying so makes us bigots in the eyes of the headless humanists, then so be it. We know the truth." Tom smiled as he reached the intersection of Royce and Route 53.

How many times would he have to investigate weredeer sightings before Wendy and Sara believed they weren't real? It was amazing how the *Babbler's* staff were so committed to its worldview. How could Wendy believe it as well? Having read the same books and followed the same blogs as Tom, even attended conventions years before him, how could she possibly believe in the paranormal?

When Tom reached the intersection of North Ashbury and Boughton, he turned right. Despite his boredom, Tom intently scanned the neighborhood as he drove south. The houses were a mix of brick ranch homes and two-story houses with white vinyl siding. Evenly spaced adolescent trees lined the parkway. If there were deer or weredeer in the area, they weren't in anyone's yards. Tom suspected that in thirty to fifty years, the street would look like it had a green canopy. His friends from Chicago complained that neighborhoods like these made Bolingbrook feel cookie-cutter, but driving through these subdivisions made Tom feel like he was home.

A few minutes later, movement to the right caught Tom's attention. He slowed down and turned the car slightly so its headlights would illuminate the scene. Ahead, he recognized a white-tailed stag with four points on each antler. The buck, its back turned towards Tom, had its front legs perched on a windowsill. It looked strong, like one of the many airbrushed deer photos he saw in magazines and on hunting websites. Right now, it appeared to be sniffing the window. Tom opened the glove compartment, pulling out his flashlight after a few seconds of fumbling and flicking it on. To his relief, the light came on.

Tom drove several feet forward; the deer was now directly to his right. He pointed the flashlight at the buck, which dropped from the window and turned to face him. Tom shone the light at its face. The deer's eyes reflected the white glare, and Tom cursed himself for even entertaining the thought that this was more than a very curious deer. Tom turned off the flashlight, but instead of vanishing, the glow in the creature's eyes turned to electric blue.

Tom's muscles tensed, his eyelids peeling back as if by force, and his right foot instinctively slammed on the accelerator. The Echo's engine roared to life as it sped away from the beast. Tom dropped the flashlight and clenched the steering wheel, hands trembling. In the rearview mirror, he saw the deer's fiery eyes.

Instinctively, Tom turned left onto Independence Lane, tires barely gripping the road. Soon, the houses obscured his view of the deer. After two blocks, Tom slammed on the brakes and struggled to catch his breath, heart still racing. Tom noticed Trevor's video still playing on his phone.

"I'm going to be joining protesters at Humanist Heart International's congress," came Trevor's voice. Tom smiled and relaxed, reaching down to recover his phone from the floor. "As my long-time followers know, I'm going, even if the area isn't wheelchair accessible. What about the rest of you sitting on the fence? I'm sure most of you have two working legs. What's your excuse?"

Tom placed his phone in the passenger seat and looked up. In the rearview mirror, Tom glimpsed a large dark shape descending from the sky. A moment later, it landed on top of a parked car with a loud crash. The landing crushed the roof of the car, setting off its alarm. Tom closed his eyes and shook his head, then turned to look through the rear window.

What looked like an alpha deer stood on top of the car, pummeling the hood. Each punch dented the metal like a jackhammer. If it was an alpha, the photos Tom had seen didn't convey their actual size. The points of its antlers looked razor sharp, its front legs now resembling a gorilla's arms, hind legs sporting talons instead of hooves. It stopped punching and opened its hands, revealing clawed fingers that glistened in the streetlights. The creature swiped at the car's hood, shredding it like cardboard and tossing it away. The hood swam through the air before crashing through a neighboring home's windows.

The weredeer looked towards Tom's car, its eyes still fiery blue. It roared in Tom's direction, revealing a set of shark-like teeth while shaking the Echo.

Tom slammed on the accelerator. The car struggled to pick up speed, while the creature charged on its hands and feet, biting down seconds later into the car's trunk. Over

Trevor's voice, Tom could hear the steel being ripped off. In the mirror, he saw the creature with a sizable chunk of blue metal in its mouth. It slowed down as it chewed.

Tom shifted the car into fifth, continuing to gather speed. He sped past the stop sign as the road merged with North Ashbury. Behind him, the creature spit out the remaining scraps of metal and resumed its pursuit. All the other side streets in this direction were dead ends, Tom remembered: his only hope of escape was to get back to Boughton. The Echo was now up to highway speed and the weredeer was still gaining. Tom pressed the accelerator against the floor. *It has to break off at some point.*

The Echo's tires squealed as the road curved, and the weredeer slowed slightly as it made the turn, then resumed closing in. As the road meandered, the Echo barely held onto the pavement, while the weredeer cut the distance by moving straight. Boughton was now visible and only seconds away. Though the traffic was light, he knew making a left turn at this speed would be impossible. The weredeer was only inches behind.

Tom spun the steering wheel, desperately attempting a hard right onto Boughton. As he heard a car horn blaring at him, he closed his eyes. Instead of a collision, he heard the approaching car crash into the weredeer. Before the outside world tilted, Tom opened his eyes and glimpsed the creature tumbling to the ground in the rearview mirror.

Chapter 4

"*I joined the atheist and skeptical movements believing we only needed science and reason for a better world. I soon found out how wrong I was.*"
—Sakura Takahashi, "Why humanism needs a heart"

A CHORUS OF VOICES woke Tom. As he came to, he saw a night sky filled with stars, but felt the weight of bed linens on his body. As the noise of the choir rose, two streaks of light flashed past, one orange and the other blue. Strings joined the choir as more streaks followed, and though he didn't feel himself moving, it looked like he was traveling down a corridor lit by rainbow walls.

Tom sat up and the lights came on, revealing a white ceiling above him. The music stopped. He was in a bedroom with black furniture and white walls that seemed to curve.

The last thing Tom remembered was being chased onto Boughton. Were Sara and Wendy playing a joke on him? No—they didn't have the resources for a hoax like that. Not without the police or the neighbors noticing.

Clothes. Tom pushed aside the covers and placed his bare feet on the floor, his toes sinking into soft shag carpet. For the first time, he noticed he was wearing a white gown. As he stood up, it crumpled as if made of paper.

Tom walked to the wardrobe and pulled open the doors. Inside, he saw his clothes professionally cleaned and pressed, his underwear and socks cleaner than he'd ever seen them.

As Tom reached for his clothes, he realized his arms were hairless. Breathing quickly, he lifted his gown, finding his legs were equally smooth, his pubic hair shaved off as well. Gasping, Tom rushed to the bathroom, staggering to a stop in front of the mirror. He now had a crew cut and his stubble-free face looked waxed. Tom smacked himself, but the room persisted.

Tom climbed on the bed and stood up. Thinking that the sensation of falling might wake him up, he jumped. Instead of coming to, Tom belly-flopped onto the shag carpet. He groaned, but fortunately, it cushioned his fall.

As Tom rose, a trumpet started playing. The pounding of kettle drums filled the room. As he tried to determine the source of the music, an entire symphony played triumphantly. A few seconds later, Robert Clark marched into the room. He scrutinized Tom for a few moments, then looked at the ceiling. "Kill the music!"

The fanfare ended abruptly, and Tom stood up.

"Mayor Clark?" he asked. "I mean... Robert."

Robert looked up at the ceiling again. "Tell Reese to meet us at Skywalk 7. No excuses." He turned to Tom and smiled. "Hello Tom. They told you where you are, right?"

Tom blinked for a moment.

Robert stepped towards Tom. "What's the last thing you remember?"

"I was driving—" Tom realized Robert had just asked to meet with Reese. He tried to chuckle, but his body was still aching from the belly flop. "That was a good one," Tom said. "You fooled me."

"Fooled?"

Tom laughed for a moment. "That weredeer looked so real I crashed onto Boughton."

Robert's jaw came unstuck.

"I got it. You're working with Reese. Only you two could stage a hoax like this. Reese must be trying to discredit the *Babbler*. He thinks they'll publish an uncritical story, then he'll reveal it was a hoax. The *Babbler's* reputation will be ruined."

Robert raised his eyebrows.

"Except my car crash complicated things," Tom continued, scanning the room. "I heard Adventist Hospital had luxury suites, but I didn't realize they were this fancy."

Robert tilted his head as he examined Tom. Then he looked up and glared at the ceiling. "Ivan!"

Tom looked up. The ceiling turned black, then brightened like a screen, showing Ivan from *Skeptical World* standing in a bar. The podcast's other hosts, except Jamie, stood behind him. Ivan was wearing a Reese Habenstein t-shirt, but the text was in a language Tom didn't recognize.

"What's up, Mr. Mayor?" asked Ivan. "Or is it 'Your Honor,' or—"

"We have strict induction protocols. You obviously didn't follow them."

"We always haze the level twos before inducting them. We've pulled off some great ones inside Area 51. Like the time—"

"This is not Area 51. Now tell Reese to get over to the skyway double time."

"You're no fun."

"No, I'm not."

The screen became a white ceiling again.

Robert turned to Tom. "Get dressed and meet me in the next room. We'll make this quick."

Robert left and Tom quickly dressed himself. He opened the door and was startled by a man in blue tinted sunglasses, a navy blue suit, and a light blue shirt blocking the doorway. The man, who towered over Tom, looked down. He paused for a moment, then stepped out of the way. Tom hesitantly entered the next room.

The room looked like a high-end apartment with an open kitchen and bar. Robert stood near the left wall, on which two metallic plates had been mounted. Next to him stood a man who looked and dressed exactly like the doorway guard. By their side were two couches facing the metallic plates. Tom hesitantly approached Robert and his companion.

Robert motioned towards the plates. "I find it's best to start with the view." Tom heard a buzz as the plates separated, revealing a window. He approached, then felt his jaw drop. Outside, he noticed a white disc-shaped craft that resembled an upside-down pie pan. Next to it hovered a blurry black triangular craft with lights along its edge. Both were the size of jumbo jets, yet lacked any visible thrust.

Tom's suite was one of several that lined the walls of this steel cave, like skyboxes ringing a football stadium. About fifty feet below him, he saw ground crews using safety batons to direct craft to landing areas. An egg-shaped vessel on the ground that resembled a Martian Colonial shuttle caught his eye. Beside it, Tom noticed a being with three arms supervising its unloading. The decorations on the being's suit reminded him of the ambassador who was always threatening to destroy the Earth.

Tom reached out to touch the window, expecting it to be an illusion. Instead of touching the glass, his fingers went numb, as if going to sleep. He jerked his hand away, then reached back out of curiosity. Again, his fingers tingled, but nothing pressed back. After stretching another two inches, he noticed the temperature was warmer on the other side.

"Don't stay out there too long," said Robert.

Holding his breath, Tom leaned forward. His head passed through the field, and on the other side, he heard a symphony of voices on the ground and the buzz of space-craft surrounding him. He inhaled. The air was still and smelled like the aftermath of a thunderstorm. A public address announcer said something in French, then in a language he'd never heard.

Tom scanned the chamber again. It all felt so real. He was in a place that he had stopped believing in long ago.

Tom pulled his head back into the room and then looked at Robert, who nodded.

"Now do you understand?"

"My God," Tom heard himself say.

"Common reaction," Robert replied bluntly. "Do you remember everything you read in the *Babbler*?"

Tom nodded.

"Not much has changed in twenty years. Clow is still the largest urban UFO base in the world—and it's my base."

Tom looked back at the landing bay. The *Babbler* was telling the truth, at least about Clow Base. He remembered all the times he'd debunked the base's existence. The arguments were sound, yet here he was.

Robert cleared his throat.

"It's like being in an Asimov novel," said Tom.

Robert shook his head. "Not enough robots. Let's go."

Tom followed Robert as the men in blue escorted them. They left the suite and walked down a metallic corridor. Tom meandered down the hall, examining everything. The air smelled sterile and felt cool, but Tom couldn't hear any fans running: they were the only beings making any sound. As they approached a black door, two more men in blue entered the hall and approached Tom. He rushed to catch up with Robert.

"So the *Babbler* was writing the truth all this time?"

"Mostly," Robert replied.

"And the other conspiracy theories?" Tom felt sick as he reflected on the ideas he'd come across over the years.

"Most of the ones you've read about outside of the *Babbler* are bunk," Robert said, maintaining his pace. "Made up by fools and antisemites who didn't know what they were talking about and couldn't stop talking about it. After I'm done with Reese, he can explain."

Robert kept walking towards the door at the end of the hallway. It slid open, revealing a tall and familiar man.

"Hello, Tom," said Reese. "It's been far too long."

Robert marched up to Reese with his two men in blue. "You didn't do a proper orientation."

"Your weredeer problem complicated things."

Robert looked up at Reese. "A problem that you brought to my village."

"We're solving it today," said Reese. "Robert, this may be hard for you to understand, but you can't solve every problem by throwing a Hawking grenade at it."

"It doesn't look as if you're solving it. It looks as if you've lost control."

"In my business, perception is a funny thing. Look, give me some time with Tom. We'll meet you at the skybox."

"I hope you know what you're doing." Robert frowned, then walked away with the men in blue.

Reese motioned for Tom to approach. As he did, he looked out through the skyway's transparent walls. Outside, he saw rows of buildings. Some resembled ordinary office blocks. Some looked like Art Deco concept drawings brought to life. Others seemed entirely alien.

"Beautiful, don't you think?" asked Reese.

Tom stepped closer. "What is this place?"

Reese put a hand on Tom's back, then started pointing at the buildings. "It's called Embassy Row. Earth's secret societies built the plain buildings. Aliens built the rest. I don't visit Clow that often, but when I do, I always like to visit this skyway. Can you guess why?"

"You have an alien boyfriend who meets you here?"

Reese shook his head and removed his hand. "It shows what could be. Out there is what's waiting for us. Once we're ready."

"Ready?"

"Once all humans reject superstition, all of this will be ours."

They gazed out for several seconds. Tom struggled to find anything to say.

"You know how we almost lost this?" asked Reese. Tom shook his head. "The damn hippies."

"Hippies?"

"In the fifties, we were well ahead of schedule. There was even talk about scheduling first contact for the moon landing. Then the sixties happened." Reese shook his head. "Crystals, phony mysticism, UFO cults, New Age nonsense. Even homeopaths made a comeback. By the seventies, the Interstellar Commonwealth was ready to give up." Reese looked outside. Tom followed suit. "Can you imagine losing all of this because a bunch of layabouts confused LSD with enlightenment?"

"So why didn't they leave?" asked Tom. "Wait. You started the skeptical movement around that time."

"I helped start it. If there could be a civil rights movement, and a women's movement, why not a skeptical movement? The first organization the aliens backed was the Committee for Humanism and Skepticism."

"But now you're in charge, right?"

"Now the board is in charge, but they get... guidance from above." Reese smiled.

"You're telling me aliens run the skeptical movement?"

Reese nodded. "They provide goals. We work towards them."

"But we always said UFOs weren't—"

"We said UFO *myths* weren't real. Look, Tom—superstitious beliefs are holding humans back. They either prevent us from seeing the truth or distort it. Look what happened when we accidentally discovered quantum mechanics. Phony mystics distorted it to create their own religion. Charlatans told people it was magic and offered to sell them overpriced rocks. We're still trying to clean up the mess."

Reese pointed at Embassy Row again. "The movement is clearing away the woo so humans can join the rest of the galaxy. Skepticism isn't a lie. It's a path that leads to the world you're looking at out there. It's a path humanity can follow." Reese turned to Tom. "Do you think you can help me help humanity?"

***

Tom woke in his bedroom, feeling more rested and energized than he had in years. Walking to the window, he parted the blinds. Outside, he saw his undamaged Echo in the parking lot. As he closed the blinds, he noticed his smooth forearms lit by the outdoor lights.

Tom's phone buzzed, indicating a voice call. As he walked to the phone, he noticed his alarm clock read 2:13 AM. *Unknown number.* Tom moved the call to voicemail.

Moments later, his phone buzzed once again. Tom grabbed it and saw a text message from Isaac:

Where are you?

Tom shook his head as he unlocked his phone.

At home, trying to sleep. Email me in 12 hours.

Before putting the phone down, Tom noticed the date and gasped. Had he really been asleep for three weeks?

Tom went back to the index page. There were hundreds of unread texts, mostly from his parents. Tom skimmed them. At first, his parents had wondered where he was; later, Robert seemed to have told them he was on a special assignment. He skimmed the other texts. There was something about an endorsement and his dad being in political debt. Then he noticed a message from Matthew Bennett.

> Welcome aboard what we call level 2. You have a bright future. Work with me, and you'll be a Society board member in no time. I hear you got a special upgrade too.

The phone vibrated again—another unknown number. Tom was about to put it into voicemail when the phone answered itself and he heard a familiar voice.

"We need to talk."

"Robert?"

"What's the last thing you remember?"

Tom blinked. "Remember?"

"Yes. Just making sure my people used the right settings."

Tom recounted what he could recall from the weredeer attack to his conversation with Reese.

"Very good," said Robert.

"But that's less than an hour. Why the hell am I missing three weeks?"

"Mostly sleeping."

"Sleeping? If I was asleep, why did Matthew Bennett ask me about my upgrade?"

Tom barely heard Robert say, "Jesus fucking Christ."

"Did somebody—"

"Tom. The important thing is that you're going to the congress."

Tom pondered Robert's words. "Seriously?"

"The Interstellar Commonwealth wants you to write a report about it. I need you there."

Tom felt his heart speed up.

"You're welcome," said Robert.

"Sorry. That's great, but I told the *Babbler* I'd cover the congress for them. Although"—Tom paused—"I guess they gave up on me when I vanished."

"I hope not."

"Why?"

"Because I want to know how they're getting you in."

Tom blinked. "Sara said she was working on getting press credentials, and if that didn't work, they'd sneak me in."

"Of course. And I need to know about any gaps in my security. Here's what you're going to do. You're going to go back to the *Babbler* and get assigned to cover the congress. Say whatever you have to say. When it's over, you'll tell me who let you in, and I'll deal with them. Help make this event a success, and I'll reward you."

"Reward?"

"Bolingbrook needs a staff skeptic. Right now, we have to reach out to the Society whenever we have a concealment breach. It's getting too expensive to always contract out. I think you're the right person to bring it in-house. I'll make you the highest paid skeptic anywhere in Illinois, and you can keep your blog."

"It's generous. What do I have to do?"

"First, you'll tell me who let you into the congress. Second, you'll write a report on it for the Commonwealth. Finally, you'll let me edit your *Babbler* article before you submit it. Do those things, and I'll hire you."

Tom hesitated. "Can I think about it?"

An uncomfortable silence followed.

"Yes," Robert finally said. "But keep in mind, it will really help your mother if you accept. Now, I've left records at Adventist Hospital saying you just got out of a coma. That should be good enough for Ms. Langston. The rest is up to you."

"I'll do my best."

"You'll do it."

Tom sighed. "I'll do it."

"Very good. We're going to have an excellent working relationship."

Tom was less sure.

"One more thing. Jamie Kyle will be at the congress. Leave her alone. Understood?"

Tom sighed again.

"Yes or no. The Commonwealth wants her to write a report as well, and I will not have you interfering. If you say no, I can always have you arrested for reckless driving."

"I understand." Tom felt as if he was surrendering. He assumed nobody was lecturing Jamie about how to treat him.

"Good. I suggest you write up your weredeer piece and hand it in this morning."

***

Tom rubbed his eyes before stepping out of the car. He noticed Wendy walking towards him, holding a cell phone to her ear. Tom waved.

"I wasn't sure if you were coming back."

"Long story." Tom locked the car. "Is Sara around?"

"Yes. She's expecting you."

Tom headed towards the office, glancing back to see Wendy eyeing the Echo. He tensed up, then walked into the newsroom.

Jenna was standing behind the counter with her back to the door while ten people watched her. As Tom entered, she stepped to her right, then turned to face him.

"Hi Tom."

The staffers mumbled as they exchanged money before scattering.

"What's going on?" Tom asked.

Jenna rested her elbows on the counter. "I told them I had a vision of a visit from a man walking two paths. They placed bets on who it could be."

Tom chuckled. "Okay. I'm just here to see Sara. Is she available?"

"She will be. I'm glad to see you up and about."

Tom nodded.

"Not everyone survives a weredeer attack."

"I'm lucky. And I think I owe you an apology. A real one."

"In that case, I'll accept it. What changed?"

"I guess I don't know everything after all. You guys aren't totally wrong."

"Totally?"

Sara stepped out of her cubicle, eying her cell phone.

"I'll leave you two alone," said Jenna. "But Tom, think about why you're walking two paths."

Sara sighed as she put away her phone. "Sometimes I feel as if I'm raising a second set of children."

Tom placed the story on the counter and looked at Sara. "I'm sorry about that, and I'm sorry I didn't call you. I—"

"Tom. Let me read it first." Sara took the papers and silently scanned them. A few moments later, she looked back up.

"I'm very impressed that you wrote this story after what happened to you. I respect that. I have good news and bad news. The bad news is that we already ran a weredeer piece."

"The good news?"

"I like what you wrote, and based on your past work, I'll consider letting you cover Humanist Heart. I couldn't secure a press pass, but we've made arrangements to get you in. Before I commit, I need to ask you some questions. I have to be sure before I ask somebody to risk their job."

Tom took a breath and nodded.

"First, how do you feel about being deceptive?"

Tom felt himself blush. "It's okay, as long as you tell the truth in the end. Just like that time Reese started a fake cult. He told the truth and returned the money."

"You'll reveal the truth after publication. Until then, getting you in and keeping you there will require deception on your part. Can you be deceptive for days?"

"Yes. I'll treat it like working on one of Reese's hoaxes."

"If you have any doubts, you can cover the congress from the free speech zone—"

"No! No. I can do it." Tom made himself smile. "I can do that."

Tom noticed Wendy entering the newsroom and approaching them.

"Am I late?"

"Just in time. Tom gave an excellent answer to my first question. My second is about Jamie Kyle."

She had to ask. Tom nodded.

"This is my concern. I am pulling a lot of strings to get you to the congress. I can't risk sending you there if all you do is harass Jamie and get kicked out. Tom, I don't need to remind you that this could be your last shot at being a journalist. Your punishment at the *Star* might have been too harsh, but if you threaten or harass Jamie, I will seriously consider imposing a lifetime ban on you. I know you want another chance, but I need to know I'm not making a mistake. I need to know you can be the reporter who exposed a corrupt student government, and not the guy who feels entitled to a hookup."

"I'm not!" Tom looked around. Wendy and Sara's gazes made him feel like he was being scanned. "I understand that this is my last chance," he said. "I will quote what she says if she addresses the congress. If she requests an interview with me, I will do an interview. Nothing more."

Sara nodded. "A professional interview. No matter how you feel. This is what good reporters do. You wrote a good story. Now I need you to write another good story and show me you can act like a professional."

Tom nodded.

"Wendy."

Wendy handed him an envelope. "Inside is a Golf Club employee badge. You need to wear it any time you are on Golf Club grounds."

Tom took the envelope, a wave of relief passing through him.

Sara pulled out a card for the dry cleaners across the parking lot. "Tell them you're picking up Charlie Baffle's order."

Tom looked at the card.

"It's prepaid. They'll give you four Golf Club uniforms. Don't get them wrinkled."

"I won't," Tom replied. *Though it might be a challenge,* he thought.

"Good. They require all employees to be presentable. Shower and shave every morning. No exceptions. If I can tell you haven't in a while, they can too."

Tom fought the urge to smell himself, and didn't need to touch his face to remember that he hadn't shaved that morning.

"Tomorrow, you'll need to arrive an hour and a half before the congress starts. Go to the Nest Bar and Grill and find Brian Gagarin. He's the manager. He knows you're working for us."

Tom nodded, marveling at the connections Sara must have pulled. Then he wondered if Brian would lose his job if Robert found out.

"While you're undercover," Wendy added, "we can message you if necessary." She pulled out a card and gave it to Tom. "If you need to contact us, just follow these instructions. They show how to send us encrypted messages or make a secure call."

Tom took the card.

"Keep it in a safe place."

Tom nodded and put it in his wallet.

Sara held out her hand. "Good luck."

Tom shook it. "Thanks. I'll do my best."

"Good. I want to see what you can do when you take an assignment seriously."

Wendy offered her hand, and Tom shook it. Then he walked out the door.

As he walked to the car, he recalled his own remarks about deception. Reese told the truth after his hoaxes, but this felt different. He wasn't telling Sara and her staff the truth. If he kept working for Robert, he might never tell the truth about UFOs to the public. Was his life now dedicated to perpetuating an endless hoax?

He should have felt excited that he was finally going to the congress. Instead, he felt confused. His father had taught him skepticism was about finding and telling the truth. Now he didn't know if even that much was true. At least he could take comfort knowing that he was one step closer to confronting Jamie. Maybe, in this case, a little deception was okay.

Chapter 5

"You say you want a debate. You don't. You want to force us to defend ourselves. You distort our identities to create strawmen, and claim the intellectual high ground while your followers threaten us online. But our lives are not arguments to be debunked. You don't care about the truth: You only care about winning, and we don't want to play your game. That's what really makes you angry."
—@BlockerBot, "We are not up for debate"

TOM DROVE PAST ROWS of modern factories and office buildings. Later, prairies, townhomes, and farms passed by. His father was wrong, he thought: The Bolingbrook Golf Club wasn't quite the middle of nowhere, but it felt like he was driving in the right direction.

After a few more miles, Tom reached a police checkpoint at the intersection of Rodeo Drive and Kings Road. To his left was a cornfield. Across from Kings Road, there were five stone slabs, one reading *BOLINGBROOK GOLF CLUB*. Closer to the road, a display sign read:

Closed through Sun for a private event. Welcome HHI!

Tom pulled to a stop at the checkpoint as an officer walked up to him. He rolled down his window and proffered his ID. The officer looked at him, then the inside of his car. "Wait please."

A canine officer and his dog circled the Echo. Another officer followed, examining the underbelly of the car with a mirror. When they finished, the first officer directed Tom to the parking lot entrance. Tom nodded and drove on.

On the left, rows of trees obscured his view of the Golf Club. Several yards later, the clubhouse came into view. His first thought was that he was looking at a small mansion. The sides were a mix of stone and wood veneers. Four police officers stood in the driveway, three men and a woman. *Security theater.*

Tom looked to his right and saw acres of undeveloped wetland, except for a semi-circular patch of mowed grass directly across from the driveway. Lily Cache Creek and a large retention pond bordered it. Eight men were unloading boxes and handwritten signs from the vehicles parked at the end of a gravel driveway. Tom guessed this was the so-called free speech zone. He recognized Trevor DeBruin, who was sitting in his wheelchair near the shoulder of Rodeo Drive. Tom pulled up and Trevor smiled, approaching as Tom rolled down his window.

"Nice shirt," said Trevor.

"Thanks. I didn't mean to lose touch—"

Trevor shook his head. "I told Isaac not to worry, and I was right. I'll tell him you were just working on a way in."

"If he's around, I can explain it all to him."

"He's in the area. He wants to make his grand appearance this weekend. I'll let him know you're safe."

Tom noticed a child with warm red-brown skin crawling out of the ditch, holding a computer tablet. As the child ran past Trevor and leaned through the car window, Tom saw her deep blue eyes. She looked at Tom and gasped.

"You're okay!"

Tom wondered what to say.

"*Meggy!*" came a man's voice. "How the fuck are you here?"

The girl, who Tom suspected couldn't have been more than nine years old, turned round. The man charged up, towering over her, his brown hair shaved at the sides and parted down the middle. Scabs from obvious shaving accidents marked his neck.

Meggy took a step away from Tom's car. "He's here," she replied, her voice flat.

"I ordered you to stay at home."

"I brought him here. Just like I promised. I'm helping."

"You've never helped since the day you were born. Mom's gonna find out you're here and make me take you home. You know how that's gonna make me look?"

"Marty," Trevor interrupted in a calm but firm voice. "Look who's inside the car."

Marty looked at Tom. He stepped closer and stared at Tom's face. "You're alive. Fucking A. You're alive."

Tom glanced at himself. "Yeah. I'm kind of surprised too."

"See?" Meggy said with more confidence in her voice. "I told you he would come."

"Guys," said Trevor, moving closer to them. "Why don't you introduce yourselves? He probably doesn't know who you are."

Marty cleared his throat. "I'm Marty Nowak. Founder of the Will County Men's Alliance."

Tom hadn't heard of them, but politely nodded.

"This is Meggy," Marty went on. "My half-sister. She's what mom gave me instead of a college fund."

Meggy hopped up to the window. "You read my email on your show."

The realization finally struck Tom. "You're that Meggy?" He looked at Marty, realizing he must be the brother from her letter.

"It's an honor to finally meet you." Marty looked down towards Meggy. "But thanks to the pest, I have to go home."

"No," said Trevor. "No need to leave. Meggy. You said you wanted to help us?"

Meggy nodded.

Trevor faced Marty. "Remember. On the field of battle, problems can become opportunities."

Marty nodded.

"The way I see it, an opportunity just snuck up on us. Meggy?" Meggy stepped into Trevor's view. "We need your help."

"Really?" Meggy's face brightened.

"Yes. But first let's say goodbye to Tom. He can't be late for his secret mission."

Tom checked his phone and saw the time. As he drove on after saying goodbye, Meggy waved in the rear view mirror, while Marty and Trevor talked.

Tom drove towards the entrance to the club. The officers let him into the parking lot once he flashed his employee badge, but still gave him suspicious looks.

"Next time, don't talk to the protesters," said one officer. "Robert's orders."

Tom nodded and moved on to find a parking spot. As he pulled into it, he took a few moments to scan the clubhouse. Though funded by taxpayers, the building's facade made it seem to Tom that Robert designed it to appeal to upper-class patrons. He chuckled at the thought that this was a socialized luxury golf club.

After getting out and locking the car, Tom rushed inside. To his left was a golf supply store, and to his right the entrance to the Nest Bar and Grill. Tom hurried in.

"There you are."

A muscle-bound man with salt and pepper hair walked towards him, carrying a small crate. He wore a black Golf Club uniform shirt.

"Brian Gagarin, manager. Two things. Help me move some boxes and promise me you won't fuck with Jamie."

***

Tom shook his arms after moving the final table into place. He knew he would be posing as an employee, but he hadn't been expecting to work. A co-worker, whose name Tom had already forgotten, held out a tablecloth. "Do it right this time."

Tom did his best to hide his frustration as he took his end of the tablecloth and stretched it out. He followed what seemed to him to be a meticulous process. How did he go from getting a tour of a UFO base to being stuck with this tedious job?

As Tom finished placing the tablecloth, his co-worker replied, "Not bad. Just remember, you need to pay attention to the details. Now go find Brian. He'll tell you what to do next."

On the stage, an employee checked the sound system. The screen behind her repeated a welcoming slideshow, with the occasional shift to one of the four studio cameras in the room. In front of the stage, a chandelier hung from the recessed ceiling. Along the walls, employees were preparing the tables for vendors and visiting organizations. Elsewhere, others finished placing tastefully decorated power strips on delegate tables. Humanist Heart members serving as coordinators for the congress inspected the ballroom.

Brian entered. "Robert wants to meet us all in the lobby. He says to hurry."

Tom and the other employees filed out. A few mentioned how unusual it was for Robert to address them before an event like this.

In the hallway, Tom noticed the cloth-covered tables laden with pastries and assorted breakfast items. Some had placards on expensive paper that read *"Vegan"* or *"Gluten free."* Tom rolled his eyes. He also noticed mirrored domes and oddly placed fire sprinklers. Tom suspected they were hidden security cameras.

Tom reached the lobby, which resembled a living room, except for the elevator doors next to the fireplace and reception desk. Robert stood by the front door, flanked by men in blue.

"Thank you," he said as the last of the staff gathered. "I know this has been an unusual assignment for all of you. I also know this level of security around the club is unprecedented." Outside, Tom saw a canine officer and dog walk by. "That's because we've never had guests like these before. The threats they've received are real." Robert looked directly at Tom, who pretended not to notice. "I have taken every feasible measure to protect our guests, this facility, and you. But we're going to do more than protect our guests. For the next four days, we're going to show them the best service in all of Illinois. That means I need A-plus level effort from all of you. There are silent partners paying for the use of this clubhouse. They've already prepaid your tips."

The employees expressed their gratitude. Robert raised a hand and they fell silent.

"But." Robert paused for several moments. "I will fine anyone here who slacks off. Understood?"

Tom and the other staff nodded.

"While these guests may not be as well off as our usual clientele, they are highly active on social media. Their posts and comments are free advertising for the club, so take pictures if asked. Answer reasonable questions and do whatever you can to make them feel special. These people are the key to more bookings. Understand?"

The employees and Tom nodded in agreement.

Robert touched a hand to his ear. "They're arriving now." He clapped his hands. "Let's show them our best!"

Brian stepped forward from the crowd. "Accessibility team outside now. Hospitality team, man the serving tables. Everyone else is part of the welcoming chorus. Line up by the fireplace."

Outside, Tom saw a police car drive by the entrance, its lights flashing, while rows of buses began pulling into the driveway. He felt a pit in his stomach. Jamie was on board one of those buses.

The first group entered the lobby. They seemed to Tom to be primarily people with disabilities. He noticed two blind attendees being escorted by staff. Several guests followed in wheelchairs.

"Welcome to the Bolingbrook Golf Club!" announced Robert with a smile. A man in blue performed sign language interpretation. Tom and the other site staff welcomed them as they passed by. The attendees murmured their own greetings and kept moving. Some accepted a complimentary orange juice, served in a champagne glass.

The first bus drove off and the next bus pulled up to the door. The next group entered the lobby. He recognized Paul Randall and Barqah Jogi, accompanied by the Committee's International Affairs Team and social media director. Tom smiled sincerely at the delegation. Barqah nodded in his direction, while Paul ignored him. Tom didn't care for Paul, but looked forward to Barqah showing up Humanist Heart.

After several minutes, the last bus pulled up. Robert and the team started performing their final welcoming ritual. The pretend smiles and forced cheerful greetings made Tom hope he would never work a job like this again.

Finally, he saw Jamie, accompanied by a short woman with strawberry blonde hair. Unlike their last meeting, Jamie was wearing business casual attire, and her hair was its natural brown. To Tom, she almost looked like a different person from the Jamie he remembered.

"Welcome to the Bolingbrook Golf Club," said Robert.

"Thanks," she muttered as her gaze brushed by Tom to focus on her companion.

"I disagree. We should be involved."

"I'm sorry, but when I think of UFOs, I think of that Matthew Bennett documentary. You know what he called my hometown?"

Brian took two glasses from a server and offered them to Jamie and her companion. Jamie acknowledged him and took a glass as they turned the corner.

For years, Tom had imagined what would happen if he saw Jamie again. Being ignored wasn't a possibility he'd ever considered.

"Tom?"

Tom turned and saw a woman in a purple blouse and black skirt. The strap of her purple book bag covered part of her badge. She looked vaguely familiar.

"It's been so long."

"Y-yeah. It has." Tom tried to see her badge.

"I haven't seen you at Habencon since my first year. You introduced me to Reese."

Tom's confusion turned to excitement as he made out part of the name on the badge.

"Pamela, right?"

"Yes. I know it was a long time ago."

"I still remember our dinner."

"And you were right. That restaurant was affordable."

Tom recalled enjoying their conversations more than he'd expected to. Especially when she tried to explain how some infinite sets could equal one.

"I know it's been a while," began Pamela, "and you just remembered me"—Tom felt himself blush—"but can I hug you?"

Tom felt relieved. "Of course."

They embraced, then stepped back.

"When did you start working here?"

"Seems like forever ago." His mood darkened as he remembered why she was here. "Are you a delegate?"

"Yes." She held up her badge. Along with her name, social comfort icon, and pronouns was a list of online handles.

"Wait, you're Mathgal on *SheSkeptic*?"

"Yes. I joined after my first Habencon."

Tom tried to hide his discomfort. Years ago, he'd implied that her post on the gender pay gap was misleading, then linked one of Trevor's videos. "Seems like it's working out for you."

"It is, but I should get going. Don't want to keep you from your job."

"You're right, but"—Tom glanced at the other employees—"my job is to make you feel welcome."

Pamela chuckled. "Well, I'm honored, but I think your job is to make all of us feel welcome."

"Busted."

"I won't stop you any longer. Maybe we can catch up during one of your breaks?" She glanced at his coworkers. "That would make me feel welcome, Tom."

Pamela smiled and walked off.

***

Tom felt relieved as the last bus emptied. He wasn't sure how much longer he could keep pretending to be excited to welcome the delegates. Now he was looking forward to sitting and taking notes.

Robert returned to the lobby and approached Tom, stopping to touch the Bluetooth device in his ear. "What do you mean a situation? Bring them here. Heavy escort." Robert turned towards Brian. "Get the coordinators."

Several minutes later, Trevor, Marty, and Meggy entered the lobby, escorted by two men with assault rifles and unmarked body armor. Four men in blue followed them in and stood next to Robert. A woman wearing a coordinator armband walked in and gasped at the scene.

"Is this really necessary?" asked the woman.

Robert looked down at Trevor, then turned to the men with guns. "Good job. I'll take it from here." The armed guards nodded and left, while the men in blue remained. Three more coordinators entered the lobby.

"Contractors?" asked Trevor as he shifted the backpack on his lap. "You needed to hire contractors?"

"Trevor DeBruin?"

"You don't watch YouTube, I take it."

Robert approached Trevor. The men in blue followed. "No, but I watch everything else. Is your family enjoying our forests?"

"It's been quite a camping trip."

"They can stay in the woods, but tell them to stay out of my village."

Trevor tapped his fingers.

"Why did you think you and your friends could just stroll into my clubhouse?"

"Marty and I are delegates."

He handed Robert two sheets of paper. Robert handed them to a man in blue, who passed them to the coordinators.

"You two are NewYorkJustice and ChicagoSJM?"

Trevor smiled. "Yes."

"You registered under false names and pretenses!"

Marty frowned as he stared intensely at the coordinator. "You made the rules. We're following them. Deal with it." A few attendees muttered, while the rest just glared. Marty folded his arms. "My taxes paid for this place. I have more of a right to be here than any of you."

Robert turned towards him. "And who are you?"

"Marty Nowak, Will County Men's Alliance."

"Never heard of them. Or of you."

Robert peered behind Trevor. Meggy remained crouched as she looked up at him. Robert smiled and waved. Meggy meekly waved back.

"You know Marty?"

Meggy nodded.

"Is he your friend?"

Meggy shook her head.

"She's my half-sister," said Marty.

"Is that right?"

Meggy nodded.

Robert faced Marty. "She looks like a whole person to me. Did you mean to say you're her half-brother?"

Marty started to talk, but Trevor interrupted. "While this is entertaining, we do have a pressing issue to resolve. Now we're reasonable people. We'll be happy to stay as observers instead of delegates. I think that's fair."

"Let me think about it."

Robert approached the coordinators, who joined him in a hushed conversation.

Tom turned back towards the trio. Marty stood like a soldier, his feet apart and his hands behind his back. Trevor calmly watched Robert and the coordinators, while Meggy peaked from behind him and waved at Tom, who nodded slightly, hoping no one else noticed. Robert broke the huddle and walked towards them, stopping in front of Trevor.

"Trevor, this club is village property, and as the mayor, I can remove anyone for any reason. Instead, I'm going to let you stay. Firstly, I know good members of your family, and if I throw you out now, they could cause problems. Second, you'll use your removal to generate publicity. So I won't give you what you want."

Some of the attendees groaned in protest.

"Fair enough," said Trevor.

"In exchange for your peaceful presence here, you will assure me that the rest of your family will not be on Golf Club property, or in the free speech zone. Am I clear?"

"Yes."

"If you try to be clever, or bother my attendees, I will remove you along with your friends. If I do, I will still expect your family to stay away and your friends not to try to sneak into this club. You three are the last ones to enter during the congress. Agreed?"

"Agreed."

"Good." Robert eyed all three of them. "Each of you will be escorted at all times. Understand?"

All three nodded.

"Good. I'm not in the mood for dealing with lawyers. Honor the spirit of what I just told you. If you disagree, leave now."

"We agree to your terms. From this moment forward, we are only observers."

"Excellent." Robert faced Brian. "Find a room."

Brian headed towards one of the meeting rooms. Two men in blue ushered Trevor, Marty, and Meggy after him.

Robert faced the crowd. "I'm sure you all know the harassment reporting procedure. If they give you any problems, let the coordinators or my site staff know. Hopefully, they're smart enough to appreciate their good fortune."

The crowd muttered.

***

Tom adjusted his chair, making sure his head wasn't blocking the camera. He'd already plugged in his phone, and had a strong Wi-Fi signal. He was ready.

The crowd, though smaller than the ones he'd seen at Habencon, was larger than he expected—maybe several hundred people, Tom guessed. It was certainly one of the most diverse crowds he'd seen at a secular convention. He had to remind himself he was in enemy territory.

Tom looked around the room again. Tables staffed by visiting organizations and vendors lined the walls. *SheSkeptic's* table had the heaviest traffic, especially when Jamie sat at it. The Committee for Humanism and Skepticism seemed to Tom to be the next busiest.

Tom noticed Robert sitting in a corner, alongside two men in blue. Occasionally, he'd tap the Bluetooth device in his ear.

Four uniformed police guarded the entrance to the ballroom, two on each side. Three officers patrolled among the crowd. As they walked by, some delegates appeared on edge.

On stage, a woman walked up to the podium, pounding the gavel on the sounding block. She identified herself as the chair and urged the delegates to take their seats.

As the delegates shuffled into place, Trevor, Marty, and Meggy entered the ballroom, escorted by two men in blue and two armed officers. As they browsed the vendor tables, Trevor spoke to the woman at the jewelry stand, who flipped him off. Marty and Trevor laughed, and made their way towards the stacks of unused tables and chairs at the back of the ballroom. Marty loudly pulled out two tables and started setting them up, while Trevor pointed to a stack of chairs and Meggy removed two of them. An officer approached Trevor, setting a power strip on one of the tables after Marty finished arranging them. Trevor spoke to the officer while Marty and Meggy sat down. After a few seconds, the officer nodded and walked away. Trevor moved next to Marty, and placed his backpack on the table. Marty folded his arms.

The screen above the stage switched to a live shot of the podium, a small window showing another coordinator.

"Please be seated," said the chairwoman as her colleague signed her words. After waiting several seconds, she reintroduced herself and welcomed the delegates. "Thank you for coming here today. You know, despite the harassment, despite the whining, despite the threats of violence, we made it. We've gathered to discuss our future, and the trolls are powerless to stop us. Your presence here is a victory for social justice in the movement. All of you are a part of that victory. Give yourselves a hand."

The audience politely applauded.

"Since Sakura's first post, they have attacked us for advocating feminism and anti-racism. They called us divisive because we believe the atheist and skeptical movements should be more diverse. But—"

A screech of feedback filled the ballroom. Tom turned and saw Trevor holding a megaphone.

"That's inappropriate," said the chairwoman.

"Excuse me," replied Trevor. Tom started streaming from his phone.

"It figures that a man would interrupt."

Trevor waited a few moments. "I just have to say something very important."

"Of course you do."

Some in the audience laughed. Others started applauding.

The officers escorting Trevor started towards him, but stopped when Robert raised a hand.

Trevor continued. "Look at all of you. You claim to be skeptics, but you act like a mob. Are you rationalists, or witch hunters?" Two more armed officers walked in.

"Are you done?" asked the chairwoman.

Marty stood up and grabbed the megaphone. Trevor reached, but Marty turned his back and walked around the table.

"I'm gonna say what my friend can't. The women here are disgusting. Disgusting *liars*. Smearing the reputations of our thought leaders with your ridiculous accusations. Why? Because they wouldn't hook up with you? Look at yourselves. Would you hook up with you? I don't even want to rape you."

The audience started booing. Some delegates stood up and started yelling back.

Marty started pacing. "I'd ignore you, but your lies are empowering the enemies of the Enlightenment. We're lighting a candle in the darkness and you're helping them blow it out."

Meggy reached out for the megaphone as Marty paced towards her. He pushed her arm away.

The chairwoman caught Robert's eye. "Security."

Robert nodded. The escorts and other officers approached the trio. After Trevor said something, he and

Marty raised their arms. Meggy's eyes widened as the officers approached.

Two officers grabbed Marty's arms. He screamed as one of them placed him in a wrist lock. The officers handcuffed Marty and started escorting him out. A female officer lifted Meggy from behind, while another held her legs. Meggy flailed her limbs as she tried to free herself.

"You don't need to use violence," said the chairwoman. "Just remove them please."

Six men in blue closed in around Trevor, who spoke to them, then lowered his arms to his wheel handles, remaining silent as they led him out. Tom turned his phone towards Meggy, who screamed and thrashed as they carried her from the room.

***

Tom covered his yawn and looked at his phone. It had been several hours since Trevor and company's eviction was followed by calls to move the congress and condemnation of the police. That debate ended with the announcement that officers would remain outside the clubhouse.

After voting to stay, the delegates spent the rest of the morning debating how to ratify any proposed constitution or incorporation document. Attendees debated whether to require a simple or two-thirds majority, with terms like "tyranny of the majority" and "veto of the strong-willed" peppering the floor speeches.

While the debates bored Tom, he felt better when he learned his video of the trio's removal had gone viral. Tom was happy to hear someone tell off the delegates at their congress, but he felt uncomfortable about Marty's choice of words. Tom also never expected to feel sympathy for an HHI member. The chair had just wanted the disruptions to end, and didn't want Marty or Trevor to be harmed. Were the police's tactics necessary, or were they part of Robert's marketing campaign?

After lunch, which featured dishes by the Golf Club's head chef, the afternoon started with more bad news. A possible financial backer and pro bono lawyer had both withdrawn their support, and the delegates now worried they wouldn't have legal support or funding to register as a non-profit. While speakers discussed this, most of the action seemed to take place on the floor of the Congress. During the speeches, everyone else broke off into groups or chatted with the vendors and visiting organizations. Tom saw Jamie and Pamela talking to members of the Committee's International Affairs Team.

"The chair recognizes the delegate at microphone three," said the chairwoman.

"Barqah Jogi would like to address the Congress."

"Second!" shouted someone.

Barqah, a woman in her fifties, walked on stage holding a tablet in a case. The background noise dimmed, and Barqah spoke softly as she thanked the gathered delegates. Paul grinned as he nodded at her. As she opened her tablet case, Tom tried to hold back his excitement, readying his thumbs over his phone. Barqah looked down at the tablet and read aloud.

"The fight against sexism is one of the most important causes in the world," she read out in a monotone. "In my years at the Committee for Humanism and Skepticism, I have heard about female genital mutilation, beheadings, women imprisoned for reporting their rapes, child brides, acid attacks, and I can keep going. Some of these things I have personal experience with. Yet Western feminists complain about compliments and adult humor." She turned towards Paul. "Blah, blah, blah."

Barqah snapped the case shut, and Tom realized the room had gone silent.

"That was what I was supposed to say," Barqah said, her voice now louder and more confident. She pulled out a Golf Club notepad with the cover page filled with handwritten notes. "This is what I want to say."

Tom looked at Paul, who was now talking to the other team members.

"When I was growing up in Pakistan," Barqah began, "I heard how fortunate I was that I didn't live in Afghanistan. Women in Afghanistan are told how fortunate they are that they don't live in Iran. Iranian women are told they are lucky they don't live in Saudi Arabia. Saudi women are told how fortunate they are that they don't live in the United States, where they can be raped because of the clothes they wear. US women are told how fortunate they are not to live in Pakistan or Afghanistan. The cycle goes on and on. I'd like to break it.

"The leaders of our community feel that abolishing religion will end misogyny. It will not. As all of us gathered here know, misogyny is still misogyny, whether committed in the name of Muhammad, Christ, Buddha, or Bennett. We must still oppose it."

A few delegates applauded.

"For too long, the Committee used my narrative not to empower women around the world, but to disparage women in the West. It has been used to shame women in our communities." She turned back towards Paul. "When powerful men abuse women, our leaders have done nothing. Instead, they enforce a code of silence and slander the victims." Paul shifted in his seat. "For too long, I accepted that silence to support the cause of secularism. No more. There is no cause important enough to tolerate sexism."

More delegates applauded. Some female delegates cheered. Barqah faced them.

"Members of this Congress, I support your mission, the International Affairs Team supports your mission, and there are others in our midst who support your mission. I have listened to your speeches and spoken to many of you. Your cause is worthy and your goals are essential. Many of you want to transition Humanist Heart from an Internet forum to a worldwide body, and we can help."

Paul looked at his fellow members. One stood and walked towards Barqah. Two more followed.

"We have legal experts who will work pro bono. We have donors who will make substantial contributions. Our contacts around the world would love to work with an inclusive secular organization."

Three more committee members, two men and a woman, joined Barqah on stage.

"Rationalism is not enough. You want to work for a better world. May we help you?"

The rest of the International Affairs Team left the table, leaving Paul by himself. The delegates stood and cheered as the rest of the team took to the stage.

Barqah turned towards Paul. "On behalf of the International Affairs Team, we quit, and we're taking our donors with us."

The former team members raised their arms and clasped their hands together, while Paul looked down at the table and shook his head.

Tom looked at Jamie. She was smiling and clapping.

Chapter 6

"I joined the skeptical movement to fight irrationality. I never dreamed that I would have to fight it within the movement. Sadly, we have to confront a modern feminist clique attempting to tear our movement apart, one false accusation and one unreasonable demand at a time. This is a challenge that requires a response. I am no longer content to be a butterfly flapping my wings, hoping for a hurricane. I must become the hurricane."
—Tom Larsen, "What happened to the *Skeptical Butterfly?"*

"Hey @barqahjogi! I know where you live."
—@StoicSkeptic79

"HEARING NO OBJECTIONS, I declare this meeting adjourned."

Tom frowned as he watched delegates gather around Barqah. Paul had long since packed up the Committee's table and left. Without the international team or their donors, it would surely have to be dissolved. Tom regretted ever disliking Paul; what little sympathy he had for Humanist Heart had evaporated along with his respect for Barqah.

Tom's phone vibrated. Trevor was streaming from the free speech zone. On screen, tears streamed from Meggy's eyes.

"If you saw what happened," narrated Trevor from behind the camera, "you saw the Bolingbrook Police Department act on behalf of radical feminists. Bolingbrook, these outsiders have turned your police into feminism's royal guard."

Marty entered the shot and approached Meggy. "I tried to reason with them, and they hurt my favorite sister." Meggy looked up at him for a moment, then tightly embraced him. "I'm through reasoning with them."

Trevor pointed the camera at himself. "This congress is only the beginning. Feminists are plotting not only against the secular movement but against every community. They want to impose safe spaces. It doesn't matter if you're an atheist or a believer. If our movement falls, it will only be the beginning. They will keep going for your schools, your workplace, your hobbies, and they will not stop until they control your life."

"Help us hold the line," Marty pleaded off-camera.

Trevor nodded. "Marty's right. I am sending a distress signal to men and women everywhere who support reason and freedom. We must come together. Join us outside the Bolingbrook Golf Club and take a stand. Show them we'll resist their headless humanism."

Trevor trained the camera on Meggy. "Look at the camera," commanded Marty. Still clinging to him, she turned to face Trevor, who cleared his throat.

"Meggy, do you have something to say to Humanist Heart?"

"I think you guys suck." She closed her eyes and pressed her head against Marty. "You called me your favorite sister."

Trevor turned the camera back on himself. "There you have it. Join us at the Bolingbrook Golf Club tomorrow for the next great rally for civil rights."

Tom looked up from the screen to see Robert approaching him, flanked by two men in blue. He stopped when his feet were less than an inch from Tom, frowning as he peered down at him.

"I told you not to cause trouble."

"Trouble?" Tom replied as he felt his face turn warm.

"Your video created a PR situation," Robert replied. "Now I have to clean up your mess."

"But you said to report on the conference. I thought a video—"

"I said *write* a report," Robert snapped back. "Obviously I wasn't clear, so consider this your warning. Do you know about the tools the NSA uses to track people on the Internet?"

Tom nodded.

"Toddler toys compared to what I have. If I catch you posting anything online during this conference again, Reese won't like what I do to you." Robert smiled. "But you're not going to create any more problems for me. Right?"

Tom looked away from Robert. "Right."

"Good job. Because I want you to remain a functional adult when this is over with. You can't be the village skeptic if you can't talk."

Tom nervously chuckled. "Won't happen again."

"That's the spirit. See you tomorrow. Don't be late."

As Robert and his escorts walked out of Tom's line of sight, he saw Pamela walking towards him.

"I hope you're not in trouble."

Tom shook his head. "Robert just wanted to clarify something. I'm fine."

"That's a relief. What did you think of the first day?"

"It was... eventful."

Pamela nodded. "Barqah came through for us. Jamie's work paid off."

"Jamie?"

"Yeah. Jamie found out Barqah was fed up with Paul's public comments and felt like he was using her. Especially after that guy hit on Jamie."

Tom felt as if he'd been hit by a falling icicle. He quickly recovered and politely nodded.

"It's odd. What he did was one thing. But the reaction by the leadership is something else."

Tom nodded again. He couldn't bring himself to argue with Pamela. He'd had fantasies of arguing with anyone associated with Humanist Heart, but Pamela wasn't like the people he imagined.

"Anyway, I think Barqah will be happy with us. Now we just have to focus on starting an NPO. There's still going to be some resistance from the forum-only faction."

Tom felt his phone vibrate and fished it out of his pocket. He had a message from Trevor.

> *Dinner with the resistance? We'd really love to have you. Bailey's Family Restaurant in half an hour.*

"Tom?"

Tom looked up.

"Do you want to get dinner? We have so much catching up to do."

The idea of more time with Pamela excited Tom. Then he looked back down at his phone, and his heart sank.

"I can't tonight."

Pamela blinked, tilting her head down. "Oh."

"But we can tomorrow. Absolutely tomorrow. There's a place in town that serves deep-dish pizza. You can't visit Chicagoland without trying it."

Her expression brightened as she faced Tom. "Sounds tempting. I've never tried it."

"Then you've never tried real pizza," said Tom. To his surprise, he felt happier after saying that. "Tomorrow, okay?"

Pamela grinned. "Tomorrow."

***

Tom wasn't sure how many times he'd eaten at Bailey's, but he'd never seen a ruckus of diners like the one in front of him. The servers' station divided the dining area in half, and on one side, the protesters' tables formed a column down the length of the room. Many protesters were furiously typing at their laptops.

Marty, Trevor, and Meggy sat in one of several booths along the wall. Trevor sat in his wheelchair, leaving a space for Tom. Meggy looked up from her spaghetti and waved, before returning to her meal. Trevor waved Tom over.

"Thanks for inviting me," said Tom as he sat down.

"No. Thank you for coming."

Meggy looked up at Tom and grinned.

"Wipe your face," Marty commanded. "You're not a baby any more."

Meggy obeyed, and Tom winced momentarily.

"Welcome to the mess tent," Marty told him.

"I got your message," said Trevor. "Your plate should be here soon. On us, of course."

"Wow," said Tom. "That's extremely generous. Thank you."

"Not at all." Trevor turned towards Meggy, who had just finished her spaghetti. "Meggy. Do you like banana splits?"

Meggy nodded vigorously. "Yes, but Mom says they cost too much."

Trevor shook his head. "Not tonight. I secretly ordered one just for you."

Meggy's eyes widened and she gasped. "Really?"

"Yes. Donations have been pouring in since your video. This is my way of thanking you."

A waitress walked up to their booth with a banana split, and Meggy's face lit up. "One banana split for you."

Meggy smiled. As she reached for the dish, Marty grabbed her arm with a frown. Meggy looked away, and then up at the waitress. "Sorry. Thank you."

Marty tightened his grip. He turned his head towards Trevor, then looked back at Meggy.

"Thank you Trevor," she said, her voice trembling.

Marty released his grip, and the waitress placed the banana split on the table.

"Just because you're finally earning your keep doesn't mean you can misbehave," said Marty. "Now don't make a mess."

Meggy lowered her head and cautiously started eating. The waitress handed Tom his BLT and left. Tom eyed Meggy's arm, looking for signs of bruising. Seeing none, he started eating, then looked around the room. "Is Isaac here?"

"No," Trevor replied. "He'll make his grand entrance Saturday."

"Too bad," Tom replied, before focusing on his sandwich and fries.

"He really wants to meet you," said Marty.

"I want to meet him too," added Meggy, quickly grabbing her napkin and vigorously wiping her face.

Marty turned to Meggy. "You don't even know who he is."

"I do too!" protested Meggy as she put down the napkin. "He wrote me."

"Really?" asked Trevor, looking up from his pasta.

Meggy picked up her tablet, traced her fingers across the screen, and handed it to Trevor, who looked down, lost in thought.

"What is it?" asked Tom.

"She's right," replied Trevor. "It is from Isaac."

"He told me two things," said Meggy. "Wanna know what?" Meggy motioned for Tom to move closer, and he leaned in. "He says whenever feminists hear facts they don't like, they go"—Meggy pointed at her head and made a circular motion—"craaaazy."

Tom chuckled. "That's right."

"It's from him all right," added Trevor. He looked at Marty. "Makes sense if you think about it." Marty shrugged.

Meggy smiled as Trevor handed the tablet back, turning her attention back to her dish. Marty looked at Trevor, seemingly unsure of what to say next.

Trevor faced Marty. "We should inspect the troops, don't you think?"

Marty smiled. "Yeah."

Trevor looked at Tom. "You can keep Meggy company, right?"

Meggy excitedly looked up at Tom, who rushed to finish his bite. "Sure."

Meggy smiled until Marty stared at her. She returned to finishing her banana split.

Tom watched as more people entered their side of the restaurant. "You've added more people since this morning."

Trevor nodded. "Thanks to your video. I hope you didn't get in trouble for recording us."

Tom paused, then shrugged. "Just got a lecture."

"Don't worry. I lost count of the number of lectures I received in the service. Just be proud that you created our best recruitment video. I've been getting comments and emails all day. The people here? This is only the beginning. Tomorrow will be big, Tom."

Marty grinned. "Soon, they'll find out we outnumber them."

"Exactly," said Trevor. "They damaged the movement today, and they need to hear our objections to their recklessness."

Tom nodded. "I can't believe what happened to the Committee."

"Barqah betrayed them," said Marty. "I still think tomorrow all of us should march over there—"

"You know we can't do that," countered Trevor. "Remember, we have to follow the plan."

"The plan is too fucking complicated, Trevor. We should just finish them."

"Guys!" someone from the main table yelled. "Barqah posted on Twitter."

"Traitorous cunt!" someone else cried.

Trevor looked at Marty. "Let's make ourselves available."

Marty stood up. "Meggy, you stay here with Tom. I'll be right back."

Meggy nodded.

"If Mom messages you, don't answer it."

Marty and Trevor left as Meggy scraped the last bites of banana from her dish. Tom opened Twitter and watched the river of text flooding towards Barqah's account. There were some reasonable tweets, but many seemed over the top. A large number tried to fill her timeline with photos of bacon and other pork products, while every other post seemed to mention rape or sexual assault. Some users directly threatened Barqah.

"Remember," Trevor called out. "Greetings in elevators offend these people. Don't hold back."

As if in response, tweets with graphic photos and illustrations appeared. Some made Tom wince. He was still angry about Barqah's betrayal, but some of the things flowing down his screen were excessive. Part of him wondered if they really were going too far.

Tom felt something prodding against his arm. He looked away from his phone and saw Meggy pushing her tablet at him. Tom set down his phone, relieved not to have to deal with the stream of tweets. On Meggy's screen was a drawing of a stick figure with a cape, with "Super Tom" written in block print next to it. He looked up and saw Meggy smiling back at him.

"I made it."

"Wow. Thank you."

"I drew more."

Tom scrolled down and saw other stick figures named after him—a soldier, an astronaut, and a spy with a partner named Meggy. Both wore goggles and black jumpsuits. They reminded Tom of the pictures he used to draw when he was about Meggy's age.

"These are great. Thank you."

She smiled again.

"You were brave today. Being grabbed must have been scary."

Meggy's smile vanished. "It hurts. More on the inside."

"On the inside?"

Meggy nodded. "Yeah. I'm not supposed to scream and shout." She glanced at Marty. "I thought I was in trouble, but I wasn't. Marty thinks I was acting. He said I did a great job. That's why I'm his favorite sister now. But if he finds out..."

Tom hesitated, unsure if he should interfere, though it disturbed him that Meggy knew the difference between fake emotions and real ones. He glanced at Marty, who was focusing on a computer screen.

Tom looked back at Meggy, who was looking down at her empty dish. "Can I whisper a secret?"

Meggy looked up. "Yes."

Tom dramatically looked around, then leaned towards Meggy. "Sometimes I yell and cry when I get hurt."

"Really?" Meggy gasped.

Tom leaned back. "Yes. It's okay to hurt. You just can't let the pain take over. Promise not to tell?"

Meggy nodded.

Shouts from the main table distracted Tom. He glanced at his phone and the river of tweets directed at Barqah.

"Tom?" asked Meggy.

"Yes?"

"Can I tell you a secret too?"

Smiling, Tom leaned forward and turned an ear towards Meggy. "Whisper it like I did."

Meggy copied Tom's dramatic head turning, then leaned towards him. "Isaac told me a girl in an elevator hurt you."

Tom felt his heart quicken. "Isaac said that?"

Meggy nodded. "He said you still hurt. So I drew my pictures for you. My mom and dad are happy when I give them pictures. Do my pictures make you happy?"

Before Tom could respond, someone from the main table yelled, "She deleted her account."

Cheers erupted. Meggy covered her ears, and Tom almost did as well.

"Today we deleted Barqah," Marty called out. "Next, we'll delete Humanist Heart!"

As more cheers and high fives followed, Tom felt his phone buzz. He saw a message from Reese.

> Come to my room at the Sky View Hotel right now.

Marty approached the table, and Tom put his phone away. "I just got called to a meeting. I gotta run." He turned towards Meggy. Meggy pretended to zip her lips shut. Tom did the same, then politely shook Marty's hand and made his way towards the door. Before he opened it, Trevor approached.

"Leaving?"

"Sorry, I just got called somewhere."

"No worries. I'm glad you got to witness a major victory."

"Yeah." Tom pondered what Reese might be about to say.

"Something wrong?"

"Not really. I mean, I appreciated some tweets, but some of them were..."

"I know. We can't control every tweet, Tom. The important thing is, we got the message out."

"Yeah," Tom replied, not feeling fully satisfied. "I guess that's what really matters."

***

As Tom walked into the Sky View Hotel, it stunned him to see so many shades of blue in a single location, from the midnight blue carpet to the bright sky blue ceiling. Upbeat pop music played from the PA system. For a second, he wondered if he was walking into an exclusive nightclub.

Tom looked around until he saw a sign pointing to the elevators, thinking of what to say to Reese. The protesters were not perfect, but they were standing up for sensible equality. That was more important than nitpicking over tactics or individual posts.

A chill came over him as he turned the corner. A few yards away, Jamie Kyle was waiting for an elevator.

Jamie glanced in his direction, and then locked eyes with Tom. For several uncomfortable moments, the two of them stared at each other.

Finally, Jamie turned and stepped into the stairwell. Tom rushed towards the door. When he opened it, he saw Jamie making her way up the stairs and started to yell after her.

"We'll talk in Reese's room," Jamie firmly replied. "Not now."

"I'm done waiting. You lied about me on the Internet."

"I said you were a jerk. You're still a jerk."

"Bullshit!"

"I'm not talking to you until we meet with Reese." Jamie steadily climbed the stairs and kept looking forward. Tom matched his pace to hers.

"Then I'll do the talking. You deliberately distorted what happened to fit your victim narrative. Your slander spread across the Internet, and you let it. You're not a skeptic. You're a grade school bully."

Jamie shook her head and continued up the stairs.

He continued. "Only you didn't expect me to fight back. You misjudged me." Tom felt a powerful rush as he released his anger. "I'm a nice guy. Really. I'm part of the Ethical Union. I've written posts criticizing Islam and Christianity. I've been a skeptic since childhood. I'm not like those other guys."

Jamie said nothing.

"How dare you? I lost a job because of you. Was that what you wanted? To cut me down and have me crawl on my knees to beg for forgiveness like some beta male?"

Tom stopped as he realized he'd never used that term before. Some of the nastiest tweets sent to Barqah had included it.

A closing door interrupted Tom's thoughts. He looked up as the exit onto Reese's floor swung shut in front of him. *Ignoring me again.*

Inflamed, Tom jogged up the remaining stairs. He caught his breath, then followed through the door. Seeing Jamie walking down the hallway, he resumed following.

"You may have hurt me, but you didn't destroy me. You opened my eyes. I learned the truth about feminists like you. I posted it. Others agreed with me. Now we're the hurricane blowing away your lies, and when it's over, only real skeptics will remain."

Jamie checked the door numbers as she walked.

Tom continued. "Do you have *anything* to say to me? Do you have *any* reasonable argument to counter what I'm saying?"

Jamie slowed down, but still didn't face Tom.

"You don't, do you? I get it now. There's real feminism and there's fake feminism. You and your friends want to co-opt the skeptical movement. That's your real agenda."

Jamie stopped in front of a door. Tom's pace quickened.

"Why won't you answer me? Why won't you engage? Do you have *no* answers? It's hard when you don't have a script right in front of you, isn't it?"

"Fine!"

Jamie spun around, her gaze slicing through Tom's bravado. Startled, he staggered back.

Jamie stepped towards Tom. "You think you have arguments? You have excuses. I never called you a rapist. I only told the truth. The truth cost you your job, not me. You think I want to co-opt the movement? I helped *build* the movement! I've been involved since I was a kid too, more than you ever were. The board is *always* giving you second chances. I've lost track of how many times they and Reese have told me to stay silent. I've lost count of how many times they promised me you'd come around. They care more about protecting your feelings than protecting me."

"Why do you need protection?"

"Seriously? Since I posted that video, I've lost count of the number of threats I've received. If you doubt me, go look it up. So let me call bullshit on *your* victimhood narrative. You're no victim and you're not a good guy. You're a tool MRAs are using to co-opt skepticism."

"I'm not co-opting skepticism. I *am* a skeptic. A far better skeptic than you!"

"You're such a good liar you've even fooled yourself! You can't tell the difference between your dressed-up misogyny and feminism."

Tom closed in on Jamie. "And you can't tell the difference between—"

The door flew open. As Reese stepped into the hall, Tom froze, and Jamie stepped back.

"Both of you can't tell the difference between an argument and a riot," said Reese.

"Text me after you've given him another chance," said Jamie. She turned on her heel and left.

Reese looked down at Tom. "Inside. Now."

Tom followed Reese into his suite. The main window overlooked the Promenade mall, which Tom considered Bolingbrook's default downtown. Reese motioned for him to sit on the couch across from the armchair he was about to sink into.

"Can you believe her?" said Tom as he sat down. "She's going to bring down the movement."

Reese frowned.

"Her group will plunge us into another dark age. We're going to lose the aliens. We've got to do something."

Reese said nothing. For several uncomfortable moments, they silently looked at each other. Tom realized he was still huffing.

"Are you finished?" Reese asked bluntly.

Tom felt a pit form in his stomach, like those he'd felt as a child before his dad's "talks." He nodded as he felt his rage burn out.

"Jason Larsen," said Reese.

Tom looked up, wondering if Reese had read his mind.

"He was one of the best skeptical activists I'd ever met. Your father was a natural at promoting science and critical thinking. He was almost as good as me."

Reese smiled. Tom straightened his head and leaned back against the couch.

"When he played the part of a cult leader, he nailed it. He was so good that when we revealed the truth, some people still believed in him. I heard there's still a group out in California that worships him."

"He never told me—"

Reese raised his hand. "He was good. I wanted to promote him and tell him the truth. I had high hopes for him. I think he would have become a great level three skeptic."

"Level three?"

"Later. The point is, your father had a future in the movement. Before I could make an offer, he told me he was going to step down. Your mother was pregnant with you, and Jason wanted to spend more time with his family. I was disappointed, but I understood. Your father's a good man. I wasn't going to get in his way, even if it was an enormous loss for the movement." Reese smiled. "I'll never forget when I got a letter from him with your first baby picture." He sighed. "When I looked at that picture, I promised

myself Jason's sacrifice would be rewarded. I was going to make sure you too would become a great skeptic."

Tom realized his mouth was open. He closed it and leaned towards Reese.

"When you became a fan of the *Babbler*, I sent you one of our first DVDs." Reese seemed to reminisce for a moment. "I'm glad it helped turn you around. You might not know it, but your father sent me regular updates after he showed that video to you. I can't tell you how moved I was every time I read about your progress. Especially when you started your blog."

"I knew you liked my work, but I didn't know you followed my blog."

"I didn't tell you."

"Why? You could have given me pointers."

"You were doing fine." Reese sighed. "Then you had your encounter with Jamie." The disappointment in Reese's eyes pierced Tom like a cold blade.

"I thought you needed some time to get over it, so when Jamie recognized you, I told her to give you some space till you came round."

"You—You protected me?"

"I gave you the opportunity to calm down. Instead, you let this interfere with your work. What's worse, you contributed to the rift in the movement."

Tom started to speak.

"Let me finish, Tom," said Reese. "I let you finish, re-member."

Tom sighed and sank into the couch.

Reese continued. "Maybe I should have said something sooner. I was just hoping you would come to your senses. Then, when Humanist Heart moved their congress to Bolingbrook, I saw it as an opportunity to resolve things. Maybe a face-to-face meeting with Jamie could cool your temper. I hoped that if I got both of you in the same room, you two could finally work this out. But here we are." Reese looked expectantly at Tom.

"Yes. But you have to see it from my side. I just invited her to my room for coffee. She—"

"I know what happened, Tom. You followed her into the elevator. You rambled a bit, then propositioned her."

"Is that what she told you? I didn't say I wanted sex. I just invited her to my room for coffee."

"You wanted more than coffee. Tom, I used to be your age. Let me tell you, back then, bumping a man's foot in the next stall didn't mean you sat with a wide stance."

Tom assumed this must be to do with sex.

"So don't pull that 'asking for coffee' act on me," Reese continued. "Both of us know better."

Tom blushed. "Yeah, but it wasn't wrong to ask."

Reese shook his head. "She was tired and on her way to bed. You treated her like a prize, or a reward for not being a wallflower. 'Showing others dignity and respect.' Isn't that what they taught you in Ethical Sunday School?"

Reese's words stung Tom. "So I could have handled it better. But she cost me a job! She could have kept it to herself, but she had to attack me on YouTube."

"Jamie told the truth as she saw it," replied Reese. "Did you even watch the whole video?"

"I saw enough to know she was unfair. I just wanted to make a connection, but she punished me by taking away my job."

"Did she? Did you ever ask why the *Star* retracted their offer? It could have been the video. Or maybe they were looking for excuses to let people go. Did you ever consider that?"

Tom shook his head. Sara mentioned layoffs at the *Bolingbrook Star*.

"I was prepared to offer you a better position in the Society, but instead, you went your own way. Now you're doing quite well for yourself. Unfortunately, your success may have serious consequences for humanity's future."

Tom waited for Reese to laugh or show he was kidding. He didn't. "Matthew Bennett is improving his standing with the level threes. You're only making things worse."

"Worse?" Tom asked. "He's one of the best intellectuals—"

Reese guffawed, and Tom stopped talking. "Intellectual? Hardly. Matthew had a few good ideas about psychology in the eighties. Now he thinks more about his dick than the future of the movement. If he gets any more influence, he'll ruin everything."

"I don't understand," Tom protested. "He's done more for humanity than Jamie could ever do. She's done nothing—"

Reese roared with laughter, slapping a hand on his chair's armrest.

"Tom, you really don't see the big picture. Jamie is vital to the future of humanity."

Tom's eyes widened.

"Her music, Tom. She doesn't sell many albums on Earth, but she's sold more songs in the Milky Way than the Beatles, Roger Whittaker, Slim Whitman, and Zamfir combined. Think about that!"

Tom only knew of the Beatles.

"You think the aliens want our technology? Our food? They want our pop culture. Right now, Jamie Kyle is our most popular export. The next fifty years of technological innovations? Thank Jamie for them."

"But you saw what she did to the Committee—"

"Couldn't happen to a more deserving group!"

Tom reeled.

"Paul did more to hurt interstellar relations than anyone."

Tom didn't know how to reply.

"The Committee is a shell of its former self. It should have died out years ago."

"But she's a loose cannon. She's out of control and she won't stop there. She'll go after the Society next."

Reese smiled and shook his head. "Do you really think she's acting without my approval?"

"You? You approve of her?"

"Yes. Jamie believes in the mission of Humanist Heart. She wants their ideas in the movement. I think they could prove useful on the Society's steering committee. Provided they agree to support our efforts to cover up aliens and the like. I expect Jamie can make that happen."

Tom struggled to believe what he was hearing. "She's working for you?!"

Reese shrugged. "I wouldn't call it that. More like we have a mutual interest in the success of Humanist Heart."

Tom stared at Reese.

"Let me explain. I'm concerned about the future of the Society. There's an opening on the board. The other members are trying to decide which organization will get it. If it'd gone to Paul, he and Bennett would have taken over."

"And?"

"That would be a disaster. When the Committee was in charge, Paul would spend hours delivering stodgy lectures. I've lost count of how many Commonwealth delegates fell asleep. Then after Bennett got into his head, his speeches went from boring to horrifying."

"Horrifying?"

"Yes," answered Reese. "Racism hidden in devil's advocate arguments. Eugenics disguised as thought experiments. Elitism dressed as conjecture. If those two come to represent humanity, their offensive views will isolate us from the rest of the galaxy. But on Earth, the Society will still have enough influence to impose their views on the world. We can't have that, Tom. And that's assuming they don't turn to the Martian Colonies for help. I don't want to imagine what that would lead to."

"Wouldn't Humanist Heart be worse? I mean, they want to impose postmodernism. You want them to have contact with the aliens?"

Reese shook his head. "Some Commonwealth leaders are pure rationalists. Most, however, represent cultures with values much closer to Humanist Heart's."

Tom shuddered.

Reese went on. "Having Humanist Heart on board will reassure them humans are on the right path. Yes, the board will have to endure a few lectures on privilege. Other than that, I often find myself agreeing with them."

Tom stared at Reese. "You can't be serious."

"I am. This rift is hurting the movement and holding back humanity. It helps no one, except the would-be philosopher kings, and trust me, you don't want them in charge of it all. Together, we can close this rift."

Tom fought the urge to roll his eyes.

"Robert told you the Commonwealth wants a report about the congress, right?"

"Yes," Tom replied. "After the congress, I'm going to tell them exactly what I think of Humanist Heart."

"Oh no you won't."

Tom tilted his head back. "But if I disobey Robert—"

"You won't be disobeying him."

Tom furrowed his forehead.

"You wanted to be a reporter, remember?"

Tom nodded.

"Then write a report. Not an editorial. Not a work of propaganda. An actual report. That's what they want. I need you to do your best to write what the delegates are debating, and what their real agenda is."

"Of course."

"Don't try to slip one by me, Tom. You need to treat this report like a news story. That means setting aside your agenda and *listening* to delegates. Listen to them like a skeptic, not a denialist."

"I am a real skeptic," Tom protested.

"I disagree," Reese replied. Tom started to speak, but Reese raised a finger. "I've read your recent work. I only hear you talking to people who agree with you and make you feel good. You say things that make your audience feel good. But"—Reese pointed at Tom—"what feels good isn't always good for you."

Tom bowed his head.

"I know this task won't feel good," Reese went on. "But it will be good for you."

Tom closed his eyes and nodded, feeling the sting of Reese's criticism.

"Can you do that?" Reese asked.

After a few moments, Tom reluctantly raised his head. His throat tightened as he pondered his answer.

"Tom?"

"I never realized how much I meant to you," Tom said, his voice cracking from the stress. "I never realized how much my family meant to you, or how much my dad meant to the Society."

Tom looked up for a moment, then looked at Reese, who narrowed his eyes.

"I will do my best to set aside my bias and write an objective report. If my report is flawed, I will be open to edits."

Reese eyed Tom critically before nodding.

"You're my inspiration," said Tom. "If I've failed you, I want to do my best to make up for it. If—"

"You haven't failed me," Reese replied. "You've made mistakes, but you'll only fail me if you don't recognize and correct them."

Tom swallowed his urge to protest.

"This is a good start," Reese added. "I look forward to reading your report."

Tom smiled nervously.

"Did Robert offer you a job in exchange for this assignment?"

"Yes," Tom replied. "He wants to hire me to be the village skeptic."

"I'm not surprised," Reese replied. "It's up to you if you want to keep working for him. I'll just say this: If you don't want to, I can find a position for you in the Society."

Tom didn't hide his excitement.

"But," Reese continued. "Write a real report first. Then you can make your choice."

Tom felt himself smile. "It's good to know that I have options."

"You always have options. Remember that." Reese stood up. "I think we're done for tonight."

"Really?"

"Yes. If you want to talk tomorrow, message me. Now you've got five minutes to get off this floor before I summon Jamie. I think it would be best if you stay away from her until she's ready to talk."

Tom nodded and let Reese usher him out. He'd risked so much just to have that one confrontation with Jamie. For years, he'd dreamed about how that moment would feel. He'd never imagined feeling as ashamed as he did right now.

Chapter 7

"Sociologists and feminist scholars have criticized these charts, but have yet to provide conclusive proof they are inaccurate. Science tells us to follow the data. Disliking the results does not invalidate the findings that are the foundation of these charts."
—Matthew Bennett, *The Mathematics of Morality*

"More weredeer attacks last night. Two cars mauled near Prairie Trails Park. Five hospitalized after an attack in Winston Woods."
—@BolingbrookBabb

TOM WIPED THE SWEAT off his forehead after setting down a crate on the practice green. It was bad enough moving crates into the Nest, but moving heavy ones outdoors was exhausting.

"You can't be tired," said Brian.

"I didn't get enough sleep last night."

Brian rolled out a small generator from a crate. "You're not in college any more. Out here, you have to work hard, and your actions have consequences. Nap time is over. Time to think about the path you want to take. Go get the cable spool."

Tom nodded and wiped his forehead again. He walked over to the large wooden spool with a black cable wrapped in it, then rolled it towards Brian, who unhooked a connector and fixed it to the generator.

"You think this is hard?" asked Brian. "It only gets harder. So, think about the future now. It'll be here sooner than you think."

"Okay," said Tom. *I didn't ask for life advice.*

"No more partying. Can't have you messing up. Right?"

"Right," Tom said, trying to stay out of trouble.

Tom started unspooling the cable as he walked towards the line hooked up to the clubhouse.

"Once you've connected the cable," directed Brian, "go back to your station and don't talk to the protesters. Robert told me to remind you."

Tom stopped himself from shaking his head and turned to Brian. "I won't!" Tom didn't know what they were building, but assumed it had to do with the congress—lighting for an outdoor ceremony, he guessed. He connected the cables, then headed for the clubhouse. In the distance, he could make out the sound of a protester speaking through a megaphone, followed by the occasional cheers of the crowd.

The shame of last night still lingered. He still couldn't believe Jamie's music was Earth's biggest export, and he also felt the pressure to write an unbiased report.

Watching the Twitter campaign against Barçah had rattled his confidence. Even after sleeping on it, he had doubts about Trevor and Marty's tactics. Should they have done more to rein in their followers?

But shouldn't Jamie, too? Undercutting the Committee was also excessive and damaging. Just because Trevor and Isaac weren't perfect didn't mean Jamie and Humanist Heart were. Maybe both sides were wrong in different ways. Tom also wondered why Isaac told Meggy about what happened in the elevator. Why burden a child like that?

The protesters' cheering interrupted Tom's thoughts and he walked to the front of the clubhouse. Brian and Robert had told him he couldn't talk to them, but had said nothing about listening.

As Tom moved closer to the crowd, he began to hear what the speaker was saying. "We have cowered too long," the man said through the megaphone.

When he turned the corner, Tom saw over a hundred protesters in the free speech zone—more than had dined at Bailey's. Across the street, the speaker stood on a stage of upturned milk crates. In front, five men wearing white gis embroidered with logos were performing what Tom recognized as a beginners' Taekwondo form. The police officers guarding the Golf Club were sitting in the shade or in their air-conditioned cars.

The speaker held up the megaphone. "We're done holding back!" The five men threw synchronized punches and ki'happed. They stood motionless, fists pointing at the clubhouse. "This is real power. Get used to it." The men broke their poses and rejoined the crowd, who followed the speaker's chant: "MRA! All the way!"

Tom recognized various YouTube personalities streaming from the event. Near the edge of the crowd, Trevor was directing volunteers at the water and sack lunch stations. He noticed Tom and waved. Tom nodded, hoping not to draw too much attention to himself.

Tom noticed he was now between the Golf Club's two fountains, and approached the one closest to Rodeo Drive, enjoying the cool mist from the dancing water. Moments later, he heard two sets of footsteps behind him and turned. Pamela and another attendee in a blue layered skirt approached. Pamela nodded and smiled at Tom.

"Hi," Tom murmured, then turned his attention back to the protesters.

Across the street, the crowd cheered as Marty marched towards the stage, pulling Meggy with him. Even at this distance, Tom could see Meggy's exhaustion. The protesters started chanting her name as Marty lifted her onto the stage with him. Marty picked up the megaphone and motioned for the protesters to stop chanting.

"Meggy has something to say," he announced.

Marty lowered the megaphone to Meggy's face. She silently looked at the protesters.

Marty leaned down and spoke into her ear.

"Thank you," Meggy said wearily.

The protesters roared. Marty grabbed Meggy's shoulders and turned her to face the Golf Club. She saw Tom and weakly waved. Tom waved back, then stopped, not sure how Pamela and her friend would react.

Marty raised the megaphone to his face and started chanting, "You can't hide." The protesters joined in. A few seconds later, Marty stopped chanting, and the protesters quietened down. Tom only saw one adult woman among them.

"My sister is the future. And she's on our side."

Meggy rubbed her eyes as the protesters cheered.

"You know, her mother tried to ground her." The crowd booed. "What did you tell her, Meggy?" Marty lowered the megaphone to her mouth.

"You can't ground me," said Meggy as if she had the line memorized. "I'm a brave hero."

The protesters cheered and whooped.

Marty pulled the megaphone away from Meggy. "So. Are we headless humanists?"

"No!" shouted the crowd.

Marty spun back towards the clubhouse. "We're not headless. Which means we can think. And I thought maybe we have this all wrong. Perhaps if we talked this out, we could settle this once and for all. What do you say? Anyone up for a conversation?"

Pamela and her companion just shook their heads.

"Just like I thought," said Marty. "You can't debate us, so you're trying to replace us." He pointed at Pamela's companion. "Look at that guy. He thinks he can be a girl if he wears a skirt." Marty pointed back at Meggy. "My sister's wearing shorts. Does that make her a boy? Is that why you ordered the cops to throw her out?"

The protesters laughed. Tom felt another pit form in his stomach.

"I'm genderqueer," muttered Pamela's companion. "Assholes."

Meggy tugged on her brother's slacks. Marty instinctively raised his free hand, but stopped. After Meggy whispered to him, Marty nodded, then lowered the megaphone to her face.

"Listen to Tom!" she said. "He's smart."

Tom saw the grin on Marty's face as he whisked the megaphone away from Meggy and looked at him.

"Great idea Meggy. You guys over there. You think you're in the rationalist movement? Standing next to you is a real rationalist! He's the person behind *Skeptical Hurricane*!"

Tom felt himself blush from embarrassment.

"He'll explain chromosomes to you."

Pamela's companion looked at Tom. "Well?"

"I'm not with them."

"They seem to be with you."

"Oh no," said Marty. "I think those two freaks are about to get blown away! Don't go easy on them."

Tom hated the way Marty referred to Pamela and her friend. Worse, Tom thought, they were treating him like a hero.

"We're behind you, Tom," said Marty. "Let's cheer him on." Marty turned to the protesters and started chanting, "Facts aren't feminist!" The protesters joined in the chant. Marty turned towards Tom and raised his fist.

Tom turned away from Marty and the protesters to look at Pamela, who looked back in silence. After a few uncomfortable moments, Tom turned and walked back into the clubhouse.

***

Tom's job was to guard one of the ballroom's cameras, but he wondered if someone should guard him instead. Throughout the morning, he noticed delegates either staring at him or pointing him out to coordinators. He wondered if they knew about the protesters praising him earlier, or would convince Robert to remove him.

Tom turned his focus to the floor debate. If he was going to be removed, he needed to learn as much as possible about Humanist Heart first.

"Again," complained a delegate, "why do we need an NPO? Why do we have to be like them? Do we really need to create a liberal version of the Habenstein Society? Let's stick with the forum. It works."

"Thank you," said the chairwoman. She scanned the room. "The chair recognizes Pamela Gorman."

"Thank you," Pamela replied, taking the microphone from its stand. "I too don't want a liberal Habenstein Society. I don't want to destroy the Habenstein Society, or control the movement. I don't want to be told what to think by some unelected board."

Tom caught himself nodding. A few delegates clapped.

"I enjoy reading the forum, and I agree it can help organize events. It helped organize this congress. But it's not enough. We need more structure if we want to succeed. Those people outside? They're organized and they're relentless. They're controlling the narrative. It's not just Trevor and his YouTube buddies leading this. Some of the most powerful men in the movement are backing them. Men like Bennett and Paul Randall. They're providing these protesters with platforms and funding."

Some audience members spoke up in agreement.

"We don't have to choose between being led by philosopher kings or a disorganized forum. We can create a democratic organization whose leaders are accountable to the members. If we don't create a more structured organization to advance progressive secularism, they will win. We could even lose the forum. Please. Please let us end this congress with at least the beginnings of a non-profit charter. Thank you."

Tom picked up his phone to start typing notes. This was the debate that had been raging all morning—one that surprised him. For years, Tom believed Humanist Heart was a united effort to take over the secular movement. He now saw Wendy was right about the true mission of the congress after all. Tom also understood why Reese might agree with some of their points. How, Tom wondered, was he so wrong about Humanist Heart?

As he finished his notes, Tom got a message from Sara.

> Cover the story. Don't be
> the story. I'm going to
> turn off my phone and
> watch my daughter's game.
> I'd better not read any-
> thing about you when I
> turn it on again.

Tom typed a reply but got an error message. He remembered being told Wendy and Sara could send him secure messages. *Save it for a real emergency.*

"You."

Tom noticed one of the coordinators approaching him. He forced himself to smile.

"Hey. You might want to step aside so you don't block the shot."

"You thought no one here would recognize you?"

"Recognize me?"

"You don't look like much of a hurricane to me."

Tom nervously chuckled.

"We're watching you." She glared at Tom.

"I'm watching too. And learning. It's not what I expected. Seems like you guys have moderated a little since Sakura posted—"

"Haven't you done enough to her?"

"Huh?" Tom replied. He'd penned posts critical of Sakura, but they were mild compared to what he'd seen online.

"Don't play coy," she continued. "You know why you haven't been fired?"

"You can't fire a government employee over their political beliefs?"

"The mayor spoke to you, didn't he?"

Tom gritted his teeth, resisting the urge to correct her.

"Jamie said it would only create more problems for her if you were fired. She's got enough to deal with already."

Tom found himself nodding.

"Brian will deal with you if you act up. I'm pretty sure you don't want that. Got it?"

"Got it," Tom replied as he imagined what Brian might do.

The woman stepped back. "Good. And by the way: facts are feminist. Fuck you."

As she walked off, Tom imagined Reese and other board members pressuring Jamie to ensure that he wasn't removed. That would be a valid reason for her to resent him, Tom thought.

Several minutes later, the congress broke for lunch. Tom opened Twitter and scanned the hashtags for the event. Anti-feminist tweets flooded his screen. It was almost impossible to read what the attendees and their allies were saying.

"Tom?"

Tom looked up and saw Pamela coming towards him. He put his phone in his pocket. "Hello." Tom didn't know what to add.

"I have something to show you."

"Okay," said Tom. "Something good?"

"You'll see."

Tom stood up and started walking with Pamela.

"I learned a lot today," said Tom. He noticed a few of the delegates side-eyeing him.

"Good," she replied, then looked ahead.

They left the ballroom and made their way along the hallway. Tables filled with sack lunches lined the other wall, and the delegates in the hall seemed more interested in their lunch than him.

"Where are we going?" he asked.

"It's a surprise."

Tom wondered if it was a good or bad surprise.

After a few more yards, Pamela walked up to a door labeled "Rose Garden Patio" and opened it.

Warm humid air greeted Tom as he looked outside. Instead of a rose garden, he saw a white brick patio with stone planters around the edges. None of them seemed to have any roses. He also saw a covered table in one corner, shaded by a tree. On it was a Chicago-style pizza already cut in slices.

Tom stepped onto the patio. Across the street, Tom could see the protesters gathered for a picnic near the pond. Tom quickly made his way to the table, hoping the greenery and fountains would obscure him from their view.

"Brian was really nice," said Pamela. "He ordered this for us and said you could have lunch with me."

"I didn't know he could be nice." Tom glanced across the street again.

"They won't see us as long as we sit right here."

Tom nodded. "I hope you realize I didn't know they'd say those things about you. Or your friend."

Pamela motioned for him to sit down. Tom sat, and noticed that instead of paper plates, there were ceramic ones with metal utensils. The napkins, held down by paperweights, bore the Bolingbrook Golf Club monogram.

"I agree with some of their views, but I don't support their tactics."

Pamela smiled as she set her purse down on the table and opened it.

"They shouldn't be insulting you. You're not like the others here. You're—"

Tom stopped as Pamela handed him a folded printout. He unfolded it, then suddenly froze. It was his post attacking Pamela's essay on the gender wage gap. Pamela pulled out her own marked copy.

"Ask me anything," she said, as she started prying out the first slice from the pan.

***

Pamela took her smartphone back from Tom. "As you can see, even if we accept Trevor's argument that the pay gap is only a few cents per hour, that difference adds up over time."

"I see," replied Tom. "But again, I think a lot of the pay gap has to do with choices women make."

"Or are driven to make. Societal expectations can push people into making certain choices."

"I see that," Tom replied. He cleared his throat. "Well, I appreciate you taking the time to, um, discuss this."

"I appreciate you taking the time to listen."

"That coordinator just yelled at me."

"Janet? Well, you did write a post calling her an enabler of cowards."

"She's part of the BlockerBot team?"

"Yes. The Tom I remember was better than that."

For a moment, Tom reflected on their time together at Habencon. Remembering it brought a smile to his face.

"What?" asked Pamela.

"I guess we've both changed a lot since then."

"I don't think I have."

"I think so." Tom shifted in his chair. "The Pamela I remember didn't talk so much about all this stuff. *SheSkeptic* has made you more of a feminist."

"Other way around. I made *SheSkeptic* more feminist."

"You did?"

"Remember, I took gender studies in college. It helped me make sense of what was happening in skepticism. Then the other *SheSkeptics* started rethinking their positions.

That's probably the only good thing to have come out of this rift."

"But at what cost? Dividing our community and distracting it from its goals?"

"These issues can seem divisive and distracting when you're not affected by them."

"We all are," countered Tom. "I'm affected—"

Tom paused, afraid he might reveal too much.

"Yes?"

Tom hesitated. "I just think that Sakura... I'm blanking."

"Sakura Takahashi?"

"Yes, her. I just wish she'd chosen a better way to deal with this than implying the entire movement is sexist."

"That isn't what she wrote. She wrote about the sexism within the institutions the secular movement built."

"But forming Humanist Heart wasn't the answer. If she'd talked to Paul or any of the other leaders, maybe we wouldn't be here."

"Did they try talking to her first before attacking her? How do you know she didn't reach out to them first?"

Tom felt his phone vibrate. "We should head back." He started gathering the plates. "Camera can't guard itself."

Pamela helped Tom for a few seconds. "What would you say to her?" she asked, breaking the uneasy silence.

"I don't know. Why think about it? She's been off social media for a long time. Even if she was still around, wouldn't she block me if I said a word she didn't like?"

Pamela looked towards the free speech zone. Tom turned and saw a group of protesters collecting garbage. The trees obscured the rest from view.

"Tom," Pamela whispered. "Can I trust you?"

Tom looked back at Pamela. "Excuse me?"

"I can tell you something, but you have to promise not to tell anyone. Not even a hint about it online. The other delegates say you can't be trusted."

Tom's mood brightened at the idea of a chance to prove them wrong. "Yes. Yes, you can trust me."

Pamela moved closer. "Sakura is going to be here tomorrow."

Tom blinked.

"She heard about the debates and wants to meet with the delegates personally."

"Personally? After how many years in seclusion?"

"I think with her here, we can persuade enough delegates to create an NPO." She glanced towards the free speech zone. "I also think if you heard her, you'd understand what we're really about. That's why I'm telling you."

Tom started to reply but stopped. He'd promised to write an objective report for both the Commonwealth and the *Babbler*. Interviewing her would add to his credibility—plus, it would be a major scoop to print her first public comments in years. His followers might even forgive him for working with the *Babbler*, and it might be one of the paper's best-selling issues. Even their publisher might begrudgingly appreciate him.

Tom forced himself to say something. "Thanks? I'm sorry. It's so much to take in. I wasn't even sure she was... you know? And now." Tom stopped talking.

"If anyone finds out..." Pamela glanced back at the free speech zone. "It could get ugly, Tom."

Tom watched the slow growth of the crowd. For years, he'd dismissed threats against Jamie and others as exaggerations, harmless jokes, lies, or the work of religious fanatics on the Internet. After his own outburst against Jamie, and feeling the protesters' rage, Tom realized violence from at least some of them was a possibility.

"I don't want that either," said Tom. "Staying quiet is in my interest too."

"Good," she replied. "Because hearing from her could help you understand."

Tom nodded. "I should head back. Thanks for lunch, and for the opportunity."

"You're welcome," Pamela replied. "Will you be at Jamie's concert tonight?"

"Maybe," Tom replied. "It depends on my schedule. Though I haven't seen her perform in years."

"Since she posted that video?"

"Yeah. It just seemed over the top."

"I don't think it was. If you get the chance, watch it again."

Tom pulled out his wallet and handed her his business card. "Here's how you can reach me. And I'll think about it."

***

The delegates seemed as fed up as Tom was bored. It was late afternoon, and attendees were still debating whether to incorporate Humanist Heart. Tom wondered if the delegates were doing more damage to Humanist Heart than the protesters.

"Tom."

He turned and saw Brian rushing towards him. "Change of plans. I need you with the hospitality team outside. After the VIP arrives, you can go home."

"You're pulling me off of camera duty? Did I do something wrong?"

"No. I'm just sending you home early with full pay. Now, follow me."

Tom followed Brian out of the ballroom. In the hallway, coordinators politely turned attendees back towards the meeting.

"The VIP will be arriving soon. We're going to greet the motorcade on the patio."

"Why aren't we meeting her in the lobby?"

"Her?"

Tom cleared his throat to buy time. "I just assumed..."

"Too much thinking will get you in trouble."

Tom followed Brian around the corner. Several Bolingbrook police officers carrying combat shotguns stood by the door. Tom heard one of them mutter something about guarding Fort Godless.

When Tom reached the entrance to the Rose Garden Patio, his phone buzzed.

> It's Pamela. What's going on?

Tom started typing when Brian grabbed his wrist. "Later." Tom put away his phone and Brian released his grip.

Brian opened the patio doors and a blast of hot summer air greeted Tom. He saw the hospitality team gathered next to the closest fountain. From the doorway, he heard the roar of the protesters' incoherent shouts.

"My God," a female employee said as Tom approached. "I never thought I'd see something like this in Bolingbrook."

Tom reached the team and paused at the sight before him. The crowd inside the free speech zone had grown considerably since lunchtime. Many demonstrators held signs with slogans like *Freedom Not Feminism*, *Skeptics Against Sluts*, and *Dogma is Dead*. A line of sheriff's deputies in riot gear stood between the protesters and Rodeo Drive. Each deputy wielded a full-length plexiglass riot shield and club, while a commander stood in the road with a megaphone.

A line of sheriff's patrol cars in front of the clubhouse blocked the driveway entrance. Deputies, armed with tear gas grenade launchers, concealed themselves behind the cars, while Bolingbrook police officers positioned themselves across the front lawn. Tom assumed they were another line of defense.

"Jesus!" yelled a co-worker, looking at his phone. "Those thugs are blocking off Reagan and Essington! We're surrounded—"

"Why are you on your phone?" yelled Brian from behind. Tom turned and saw him approaching. "Put it away! Stand up straight. Check your shirts. The VIP is almost here."

Blocking off those two roads, Tom knew, meant Rodeo Drive was the only way in or out of the Club. This was no protest, he realized, but something far more coordinated—the work of someone with a military background. Someone like Trevor.

"Heads up," Tom heard Marty say into a bullhorn.

"Battle stations," said Trevor through a megaphone. The protesters started to crowd the picket line. "Get ready. Don't let the matriarchy cult silence you. Tell the feminists. Tell the mayor. Show the world we're MRAs all the way. MRA! All the way!"

The protesters took up the chant.

An armored car drove into view, followed by five Will County SUVs. Two patrol cars reversed to unblock the driveway. The armored car drove past the first turnoff, then stopped. A hatch opened. A deputy wearing a riot helmet and bulletproof vest climbed up and pointed a water cannon towards the protesters. As the SUVs approached the driveway, the protesters' chants merged into an incoherent roar. Some tried to push through onto the road, bending part of the deputies' line.

Tom joined his co-workers in forcing himself to smile and wave at the approaching SUVs.

"Keep it up!" yelled Brian. "Don't stop!"

Some protesters started throwing glass bottles at the deputies. Across the street, police and deputies retaliated by firing tear gas canisters into the crowd.

Moments later, Tom froze as he heard several apparent gunshots. In front of him, the officers took cover. Tom dropped to the ground. His co-workers did the same, several of them screaming in terror.

"Don't panic," said Brian as he kept waving. "Those were fireworks, not guns. Keep waving. We're almost done. No one's going to die today."

Tom looked out and saw deputies charging into the free speech zone. Through a haze of tear gas, he glimpsed a protester setting off a new string of fireworks, while the deputy in the armored car fired the water cannon at the rest. Though some staggered away, the protesters surged at the deputies, colliding against their shields. Tom heard a shot—closer this time—and turned to see a deputy pointing her pistol at the sky.

"Back inside!" Brian yelled, as Tom's co-workers scattered towards the patio door. Tom followed, staying low as he heard more gunshots. After a few moments, he stood, catching sight of a team of SWAT officers escorting someone under a ballistic blanket.

"Tom!" Brian yelled. "Over here." Tom lowered his head and made for the door.

"Fall back to the church," Trevor commanded over his megaphone. "Fireworks are free speech!"

Tom dove inside and rolled to a stop in the hallway. He noticed his hands shaking. Why were the police making the situation worse?

Brian walked in, calmly closing the door. Tom noticed a group of his co-workers huddled in the hallway. Some were crying, while others seemed to be in shock. Brian closed the curtains.

"I need everyone's attention." Tom and the staff focused on Brian. "Calm down," he said. "We're safe now. Take a breath."

Brian waited a few moments. "Good job everyone. We just showed that the Bolingbrook Golf Club is not only the safest place in Illinois, but the best staffed. You just welcomed a VIP during a riot. Right now I'm proud of all of you. Go home and get some rest. Then come back here bright and early tomorrow, because this isn't over."

Tom texted Reese.

> Getting out of hand. Need to talk.

Moments later, Reese replied.

> At Clow. Meet me at the hotel in two hours.

"Tom?" asked Brian.

"Yes?"

"Go where you need to go."

***

As he sat in his car, Tom had lost track of how many times he'd played the last few seconds of Jamie's video. He'd arrived at the Sky View Hotel early and decided to take Pamela's advice. He thought he'd only play it once, but that wasn't enough. Tom pressed replay, repeating the cycle.

In the video in his hand, Jamie asked strangers not to hit on her in elevators because it made her uncomfortable. Tom remembered Jamie saying she felt threatened by him. He remembered yelling obscenities and throwing away his *SheSkeptic* necklaces after first hearing it. Now he couldn't understand why he reacted like that. He wondered whether he was watching the right video.

After it finished, notifications about the riot filled his screen. He tapped on one and skimmed the article. It was mostly quotes from Robert bragging about the club's security, and the "brave officers" who defended the staff and attendees. An update claimed that officers had "rescued" Meggy from the rioters, with a photo of an officer escorting her back to her mother. It also mentioned Marty as a person of interest.

Tom's phone alarm went off. After locking his car, he made his way to the hotel. As he walked into the lobby, his phone vibrated. Tom pulled it out of his pocket and saw his mother was calling him. He was about to send it to voicemail, but remembered she hadn't heard from him in weeks. He took the call.

"Mom, I'm kind of busy—"

"Thomas Gill Larsen!" his mother snapped back. She hadn't called him by his middle name since the ninth grade.

"I read your blog, Tom. Don't you dare hang up on me."

"I won't," Tom sheepishly replied. He looked at the elevators and worried about being disconnected.

"I didn't want to believe it," his mother continued. "How can you defend such misogynistic—"

"I'm not a misogynist," said Tom, entering the stairwell.

"Are you saying *Skeptical Hurricane* isn't your site? Because your name's all over it, and I heard your podcast."

"It is my site, but—"

"What's going on, Tom? For the past three years, you told me you were doing freelance writing. I didn't want to pry into your personal business, but that was before you started arguing with the mayor and vanishing for weeks."

"I can explain."

"Can you explain writing posts that attack women?"

"I don't attack women! I criticize today's feminism."

"I'm a feminist, Tom."

"But you're not one of those feminists. Mom, I like women, and feminism started out just fine. Then it went off the rails. You saw the video I did about your wave of feminism, right?"

His mother didn't respond. Noticing people staring, Tom started up the stairs.

"Mom, I know there are some bad guys out there. But we can't let a few bad men excuse hysteria. This generation's feminists are out of control. They'll support Islami—" Tom remembered Barqah's speech, then paused. "I mean, it seems like they don't realize how much better things are now. They just keep fighting. You're not like that. Did you see the video where I said your wave of feminism was sensible?"

A long silence followed. "Thomas," his mother said slowly. "I don't know what wave of feminism mine was, but I will say this. When I was active in the movement, men said the same things about us that you just said about feminists now. Feminists before me heard the same thing. Every time feminists achieve something, no matter how small, they get accused of going too far. Calling past feminists 'sensible' is a tactic used to subvert progress."

"Yeah, but have you read the news?"

Tom reached his floor and started towards Reese's room.

"Yes," his mother replied.

"You know about the skeptics thrown out of the Golf Club?"

"They were bullies, Tom."

"If you saw what happened—"

"I saw the video."

"Okay. We can agree to disagree."

"No. They were bullies, and the way they used that little girl was sickening. Did you hear about the riot?"

"Of course." Tom wasn't sure if he should tell her he was there. "They were wrong to do that, but what about—"

"'What about?' Jesus, Tom, you're turning into a Republican pundit?"

Tom stopped. "What do you mean?"

"The people who do the most to hold back women, or any other group for that matter? They aren't klansmen, or men's rights groups, or militia members. It's the moderates—the ones who say both sides are wrong because they benefit from the status quo. You're parroting their arguments."

"That's not fair."

"Isn't it?"

Tom felt uneasy as his mother waited. "You're saying feminists can't go too far?"

"No."

"Well, I just think the feminists in the skeptical movement are going too far. You have to agree setting up whisper networks about guys like Matthew Bennett is going—"

"*TOM!*"

Tom's body twitched. He hadn't heard her yell like that in years. He heard his mother breathing as if she were trying to calm herself.

"Mom?"

"Did you ever wonder why I was never involved in the skeptical movement?"

"Not really."

"Before you were born, Bennett was interested in me. He knew I was married to your father, and that didn't stop him."

"He—" Thoughts that were once unthinkable filled Tom's head.

"No, he didn't. But he was very inappropriate towards me, and if the right circumstances had come about, who knows what would have happened?"

Tom remembered the woman he saw with Bennett at Habencon. His lower lip went numb.

"When your dad confronted him, Bennett threatened him. He also threatened me, and he had enough power to back up those threats. It's the reason your dad walked away from the Habenstein Society. So, I understand why there are whisper networks. Because I am one of those women."

Tom didn't want to believe it, but he knew she wouldn't make up something like this. He hurried towards Reese's room, wanting to run from what he was hearing. "I didn't know. That wasn't right."

"No, it wasn't right," she replied. Tom heard the pent-up rage in his mom's voice. "I can't do anything about him, but I thought I could raise you to be better. I didn't send you to Ethical Sunday School so you could grow up to be a cheerleader for male entitlement, and your father didn't teach you skepticism just for you to worship idols."

"I'm not. I don't!" protested Tom, seeing the door to Reese's room and dashing towards it.

The door opened, and Jamie stepped into the hallway. Tom stumbled to a stop, then took a few steps back, motioning with his free arm and hoping Jamie would take the hint and walk away.

"Then why do you have those disgusting links on your blog? Especially that Trevor person."

"What's wrong with Trevor?"

Jamie lowered her head, then walked away from Tom.

"You don't know? Tom, he encourages men to believe they're entitled to any woman they want. Is that what you believe?"

"Of course not."

Why isn't Reese greeting me?

"Then why—Oh God!" Tom heard his mother gasp. "Oh Tom. You were at Habencon that year. Are you that guy?"

Peering into the room, Tom saw Reese face down and motionless on the floor.

Chapter 8

REESE. FUCK. WAKE UP. Oh shit. Oh SHIT. Find a pulse.
FUCK. Call 911. Phone. Dropped it. Fuck. No signal. Hotel
landline. Dead. CPR. Can't be hard. Just like TV. Press
to the rhythm. Breathe for him. Come on Reese. Reese. You
can't go yet. Reese? You're not done.

Press. Breathe. Again. We can write about this. Our
first article. Debunk near death experiences. Press. Breathe.
Again. You can't go now. Too much to do. You have to edit my
report. You have to denounce the riot. Press. Breathe. Again.

You win. I'll leave Jamie alone. Quit blogging, endorse
Robert, whatever. Just come back Reese. Come back. You have
to. I'm lost.

I need you.

***

A sound from the hallway, like a digitally distorted scream,
made Tom look up. He'd lost track of how long he'd been
resting his head on Reese, and wondered whether he'd
imagined it. The lights, which had been blinking while

Tom performed CPR, flickered once more, and the room phone rang twice before falling silent. Tom looked down at Reese, then closed his eyes and embraced him one last time. *I hope you heard me.*

The lights went out again, and this time Tom was sure he heard a scream. Towards the end, it sounded human, almost like Jamie—Jamie, who had left Reese like this. Tom's sorrow turned to rage—a rage greater than what he'd felt in the stairwell, or when he first saw her video all those years ago.

Tom grabbed his phone. The signal bars were too intermittent to stream, and the Wi-Fi was down. A recording would have to do. He stood up and activated his phone's camera. Tom raced out of the suite and into the hallway, where he saw Jamie on the floor, struggling to remain upright.

"How could you?!"

Holding out his phone, Tom rushed towards Jamie, who shifted her body to sit upright against the wall, covering her face as she moaned in pain. Remembering her video, Tom angrily pointed his phone at her.

"Reese is dead, Jamie. HE'S DEAD. I found him after you left. What do you have to say?" Jamie lowered her head and curled her fingers, as if in excruciating pain. The hallway lights sputtered. "He defended you. He told me to give you a chance, and you—*Fuck!*"

In his hands, Tom's phone started to reboot. He suspected whatever caused the lights to dim was affecting it too. Jamie groaned in pain as she stood, still trying to cover her face. After a few moments, she slid her back against the wall to return to a seated position.

As Tom's phone booted back up, updates flashed across his screen—among them, a live stream tagging Pamela and Jamie. Tom tapped the alert, and, with his Internet connection back to normal, the video started autoplaying. On screen, Jamie, on stage at the clubhouse, started playing what used to be his favorite song. Tom glanced at the replies, confirming what he saw. *But if that's Jamie there—*

Before he could finish the thought, his connection failed, coinciding with the lights blinking out. Tom looked up from his phone. For a moment, Jamie and her surroundings blurred, the electronic locks on the hotel doors blinking red. Jamie's hair length and color appeared to change: Tom watched in shock as colors and textures ran on her skin, like dyes in a pool of swirling water. Her outfit seemed to glitch as new items of clothing flickered in and out of existence.

Tom stared in disbelief at what he was seeing. He remembered that his phone was still recording and started adjusting the shot. "Who are you?" he whispered, as Jamie's transformations became more rapid and pronounced. "Who or *what* are you?"

Tom inched towards the being in front of him, whose skin parted at the right hip to reveal a long-covered holster.

"You're on the Internet!" Tom lied. "You kill me, the entire world will know. Now tell us who you are and what happened to Reese." The being unsnapped the top of the holster. Tom froze in his tracks, but kept recording.

Weapon or no weapon, he had to know the truth. "Did you kill Reese?" The being gripped a black handle. Tom steeled himself. "I asked you a question. Did you?"

The being pulled a sharp object from the holster and pointed it at Tom. Across their face, features randomly appeared and disappeared, like static made of human flesh. "*Back*," they said, their voice sounding like a blown speaker. Tom stepped back and focused on recording. "*Back!*" the intruder repeated. They stabbed the object into their own thigh, screaming in pain as it glowed a bright blue, which then enveloped their body.

Tom felt his phone growing hot in his hand and static electricity in the surrounding air. Within seconds, the phone became too hot to hold. He dropped it and shook his still-stinging hand. On the floor, bolts of electricity shot out of the phone and arced towards the stranger. The nearby door locks and ceiling lights exploded, sparks drawn towards the light as if to a magnet.

The glow faded, and Tom saw the stranger wearing a full-body suit that concealed their head. They gingerly stood and limped towards the stairwell, the object still embedded in their thigh. As the stranger made their way down the hall, more lights and locks ruptured. Electricity flowed into the object, lessening their limp.

"What *are* you?" Tom asked them again.

The stranger offered no response. Seconds later, they reached the stairwell door and rushed inside. After the door closed, Tom ran up to it, holding his hand near the metal doorknob. He didn't feel any charge, but could hear the chaos the stranger was creating on the other side. Taking a deep breath, he opened the door.

Tom found himself stumbling to a stop, feet suddenly on pavement instead of carpet. He was now in the parking lot, looking out at the Bass Pro Shops and the Promenade mall. He glanced back at the upper floors of the hotel where he'd been just moments before. Hearing an approaching vehicle behind him, he turned to see a dark blue SUV driving towards him with its headlights on. Tom used an arm to shade his eyes.

The SUV stopped and its lights went off. Two men in blue stepped out, then silently moved in unison towards Tom, who wondered if there was any point in running. Tom waited, and both men stopped mere inches from him. A moment later, the man on Tom's right walked towards the hotel. The other continued to stare at him.

Suddenly, a word appeared in front of Tom, floating like a three-dimensional text message.

Report.

Tom shook himself. The word persisted. He reached to touch it, but it stayed out of reach. The word floated up, and another appeared beneath it.

Report.

Tom tried to speak. Instead, another word appeared.

What?

It was as if the text was projected onto his cornea.

Why can't I talk?

Implant has rerouted vocal function via this secure text channel.

Tom gasped.

Implant?

Tom caught himself touching his head.

Do not be distracted. Report.

At first, Tom struggled to focus his thoughts, and over-come the distraction of seeing his own voice replaced by text. Eventually, he was able to tell the man in blue what had happened. When he finished, Tom noticed more blue SUVs arriving in the parking lot. He turned his attention back to the man in front of him.

Go home. Inform no one of this inci-dent except approved personnel. Focus only on your report this weekend. Acknowledge.

"Acknowledged," Tom said, regaining his voice.

***

After borrowing two phones from his father's shop, Tom returned to his apartment. He closed all the blinds, discon-nected his router, and unplugged his PC. Then he raced to the living room.

Tom pulled out his portable stereo, then skimmed his small CD collection, pulling out the CD by the host of the *Skeptical Minute* podcast. He set the stereo on the dining room table, plugged it in, and blew the dust off the display, then popped the CD in, pressed play, and cranked up the volume. The song "Virile Vaccinated Man"—a worse imitation of rap music than he remembered—filled the room. Tom turned on the TV, adding a patriotic pillow commercial to the cacophony. He didn't care if the noise bothered his neighbors. No one was going to eavesdrop on this phone call.

Tom pulled Wendy's card out of his wallet and skimmed the instructions. Relieved at their simplicity, he turned off all the lights in his apartment except the bathroom's. He closed the door behind him, then dialed the number on the card.

A recorded greeting in Spanish played. Tom didn't speak Spanish, but he recognized the name of an old video rental store that had closed years ago. The greeting ended with a tone, and Tom pressed the numbers provided in the instructions. After a few moments of silence, there was a new tone. "It's the kind of weather a cuckoo would like," he read out.

Music started playing. Tom turned off the light, then fumbled his way to the bathtub. Pulling the curtains shut, he sank down into the tub and waited—then kept waiting. He felt like a turtle in the middle of a dark road.

Tom heard a click. "Tom, it's Wendy. Sara's with me. Are you okay?"

Tom quietly relayed the events of the day, still fearful of being spied on. He broke down repeatedly while re-membering how he found Reese. Tom worried he was sounding emotional and irrational, but didn't care—what he was feeling was too painful to hold in. Now he was reduced to confiding to the editor of the *Babbler*, a paper he'd hated for years, because Sara was the only one who might understand. Finally, he neared the end of his story.

"I don't know how I got into the parking lot," Tom said. "Like I lost time or jumped ahead." His hands began to shake. "Sorry if I'm not making sense."

"You're doing fine," said Wendy. "Now tell us what happened next."

"Then I went home. Now I don't know what to do. If you decide to pull me, I'll understand."

Tom wiped his eyes with his free hand. Panicked thoughts rushed through his head and he started trembling.

"Wendy?" Sara asked, breaking an uncomfortable silence.

"Well," Wendy replied. "Tom just confirmed what my sources have been telling me. We're dealing with hypertime rifts."

"Rifts?" asked Sara. "Not unauthorized abductions?"

"Abductions usually last hours. Tom only lost several minutes, just like all the others. It also helps explain Jenna's visions."

"Maybe," Sara replied. "But do you know how unlikely a time rift is? There haven't been any in Bolingbrook since the time invasion in 1984."

"Time invasion?" asked Tom.

"In 1984," Wendy replied, "invaders from the thirty-first century attacked Bolingbrook by engineering hypertime rifts."

"Bolingbrook won," added Sara, "by sending men in blue to the future to prevent the invention of their rift technology and stop the invasion from happening. Which means there shouldn't be any more rifts."

"Hypertime rifts can occur naturally," countered Wendy. "This traveler could be from later in this century for all we know."

"Wait," managed Tom. "You're saying we're dealing with a time traveler?"

"Probably," said Wendy. "It's the simplest explanation."

Tom felt his back slide down the bathtub wall. Were-deer, aliens, secret societies, and now time travelers. It was all getting to be too much. Then he felt his heart start pounding. "Oh shit. You're telling me we're dealing with someone who could kill our parents, or kill us as babies?"

"Fortunately," Wendy replied, "time travel doesn't work that way. Can I explain?"

Tom sat up. "Okay." He paused. "But keep it simple?"

"Sure," said Wendy. "Imagine a circuit, only instead of electricity, it conducts temporal energy. Every point on our timeline is connected to this circuit. If someone travels back in time or sends information into the past, they disrupt the circuit so much their timeline gets destroyed, and create a new timeline from that point. The time traveler is disconnected from the circuit: without a connection to it, they'll fade away—a process called temporal erosion."

"So, you're dead the moment you arrive in the past?"

"Unless you can absorb a tremendous amount of energy. But the more changes you make to the past, the more energy is required. Going back in time is a death sentence—the only question is how long you can survive."

"So what, exactly, is a rift?" asked Tom, struggling to keep up.

"Rifts are tears in the fabric of spacetime that open into hypertime."

"Hypertime?"

"Sorry. Think of it as what exists outside of time. In theory, if you built a hypertime chamber—a room outside your own timeline—you could use it to locate rifts and travel to the past and back."

"And survive your timeline being erased?"

"Exactly. Which would explain the time skips. When a rift collapses, it pulls the surrounding area forward in time."

"Like the undertow from a sinking ship?"

"That doesn't happen, but you've got the idea."

"So, time travel is limited by when and where rifts are? And by how much energy a traveler has to compensate for erosion?"

"Exactly. That's why rift travelers are so rare. Tom, if I'm right, this could be the story that makes your career at the *Babbler*."

Tom looked towards the bathroom door, his eyes now used to the dimness, then sighed. "I don't know. There's just so much to process right now."

"I understand, Tom. But good reporters can set aside—"

"*Aside!* How can you ask me to set Reese aside? He died today. Maybe he was killed. I don't know! Reese was a role model to me and so many others, but you're talking about energy and travelers and chambers? I don't even know if I should write about this, but I have to." Tom stuttered, failing to find the words to say next.

"Tom," Sara replied calmly. "You have my sympathy for your loss."

"I didn't mean it that way," said Wendy, "and I apologize."

"Thank you," Tom managed to reply.

"Wendy," said Sara. "I need to talk with Tom privately."

"Sure, but let me say this." She paused. "Like I said, I knew Reese. I remember his commitment to finding out the truth. You know, he wouldn't even have a sip of beer because he was afraid it would cloud his senses. So I want you to consider this, Tom. Reese is dead, and may have been killed by a time traveler. If that's all they wanted to do, they could have let temporal erosion kill them. But they fought to survive. That leads me to think this traveler has more work to do. Based on when these time skips started, I believe their motivation involves Humanist Heart. If you want to honor his memory, help us discover the truth."

Tom contemplated Wendy's words.

"Wendy," said Sara, "I think you need to edit Reese's obituary."

"Okay," she replied. "Remember what I said, Tom."

Wendy disconnected.

"Tom?"

"Yes?"

"Like I said, I am very sorry for your loss. I will understand if you choose to drop this assignment, but we have to talk first."

Tom shifted in the bathtub to get comfortable. "Okay."

"Is there anything you want to tell me?"

"I just need to know what you want me to do now."

"You can start by telling me the whole truth."

Tom's back slid down the side of the bathtub again. "Whole truth?" he said, pretending he didn't know what she meant.

"Like how you weren't at Adventist Hospital during your coma."

Tom blushed as he tried to think of something to say.

"You were inside Clow UFO Base," Sara continued. "We also detected the implant in your head when you visited our office. Did Robert tell you about it?"

Tom shook his head. "No." He fell silent, dreading what he was about to reveal. "Robert didn't, but a man in blue did. In the parking lot, he used it to send text messages." Tom felt butterflies form in his stomach. "If I have a brain implant, does that mean Robert is listening to us? That he can control me?"

"It's not that kind of implant, Tom. If Robert could do that, we wouldn't be talking."

"Kind? What kind do I have?"

"The kind issued to all Bolingbrook's covert employees. It lets you interact with the men in blue and access the covert computer network."

"I can log into that?"

"Only if Robert tells you how."

"Oh." Tom remembered his secret was out and sighed. "You're right. I was inside Clow after that weredeer attacked me. I remember meeting Robert and Reese. I don't remember getting an implant, or any more instructions from Robert."

Tom gasped as he had a horrific realization.

"The aliens want me to write a report about the congress. If Robert finds out I contacted you, what will happen to me?"

"He won't. And if I wanted to expose you, I'd have done that already. I want you to write this story, and that means we need Robert to trust you."

Sara's comment about Robert reminded Tom of all the promises he'd made and secrets he'd been trusted with. At this point, he was unsure whose side he was on.

"What do I do?"

"Tom. You just survived a riot and lost Reese in one night. You're traumatized and you need time to mourn. I understand that. So go get some sleep. You need to go back to the congress, but first I need you to make a choice."

"A choice?"

"Yes. I don't want a double agent on my staff, so you'll need to decide who you work for. You have your choice of paths. You can decide to work for the mayor and help him cover up Clow. It can be rewarding to work for him. He might even promote you to an elected office. Illinois politicians get great benefits, including pensions. You just have to never get on his bad side. Because if you do, he will destroy your career and the career of anyone close to you."

Tom remembered his mother's plan to run for the library board.

"Or you could stay in the skeptical movement as a level two member—one of the few who knows the whole truth about the movement. Reese may be dead, but I'm sure you could ask whoever takes his place to hire you. If you do, your web traffic will be much higher than it is now. You'll be in demand on the cable news channels. Any book you write will be a bestseller. Your speaking engagements will sell out. You'll even get to share drinks with aliens at the consulates. If you're lucky, you might get to go visit another planet. Sure, you'll also be contributing to the greatest coverup in human history, but maybe they'll reveal the truth in your lifetime, and you won't have to lie for the rest of your life.

"Or you could work for us. We still have openings. The pay isn't that great. You'll lose your online followers. Bennett and the rest of the skeptical leaders will denounce you. Most residents will treat you the way the ancient Greeks treated Cassandra. We can't match whatever offers Robert and the skeptical leadership present you with—we can't promise you glamor, wealth, or fame—and there's also a personal risk to covering these stories. But there is one thing we do offer that they can't: the opportunity to expose lies. Even if they don't believe you, you can go to sleep knowing you gave them the truth."

Tom rubbed the dried tears from his eyes.

"There are many paths in front of you," said Sara. "Tomorrow, you need to pick one."

Chapter 9

"This sales manager finished by saying, 'Perception is reality.' Seriously. This was after I showed slides of optical illusions. My answer was simple. Reality is reality. You can't fool reality, but reality can fool you."
—Reese Habenstein, "A Lecture on Practical Skepticism"

"Being mistaken doesn't make you a bad person. It's what you value that determines who you are."
—Jamie Kyle, "Why we cling to our mistakes"

TOM FLINCHED AFTER FINISHING another energy drink. He'd lost count of how many he'd gone through, but they were the only things keeping him awake as he waited for the morning to start.

Brian's phone call had interrupted what sleep he managed to get. Tom's boss had informed him that there were new security measures in place, and that all Golf Club employees needed to gather at the Bolingbrook Commons strip mall for "enhanced checks." After one more display of security theater, Tom and the employees were bussed to the Golf Club. More law enforcement officers guarded the clubhouse while helicopters circled. The free speech zone lay abandoned, still strewn with the debris from yesterday's riot.

As the delegates and coordinators filed in, they seemed too distracted to notice Tom. Some complained about being surrounded by fascist creeps and fascist cops. Others speculated about whether Sakura would still address the congress. Most talked about Jamie's performance the previous night.

Tom focused on the delegates taking their seats. Was the traveler here among them now? No one seemed out of place—then again, the traveler was a shapeshifter. No one looked pained or suspiciously close to an electrical outlet. Then again, he wondered, what could he do if they showed up? Ask for an interview?

Tom's focus returned to the here and now when he heard the delegates in front of him muttering. He noticed several studying their phones, before his buzzed.

"Reese died!"

Some delegates gasped, while others looked at their devices. A clamor of voices soon filled the room. The chair called the congress to order, then asked for silence, and the voices dissipated.

"Before we begin, I understand we're all shocked. But we have catching up to do." She watched a delegate step up to the microphone. "Yes?"

"I'd like to yield my time to Jamie Kyle. If possible?" No one objected. The delegate returned to her chair.

Jamie approached the microphone, wiping her eyes. The delegate said a few words to Jamie, who collected herself.

"Thank you." Jamie lowered her head, then looked up with a sigh.

"This is quite a shock," said Jamie. "I spoke with Reese two nights ago, and he seemed fine. But..." Jamie gulped. *It was two nights ago.*

The last time Tom had seen the man he considered a grandfather, Reese had witnessed him screaming at Jamie. Now that he knew how much he'd cared for both of them, Tom felt ashamed.

"I only had one grandpa growing up," Jamie continued. "I never knew my father, and my uncle never introduced me to his parents. Reese was my second grandfather. He stuck up for me when I started at *Skeptical World*. When I started receiving hate mail, he assured me I belonged on the show. When I doubted my singing ability, he encouraged me to keep going. 'The universe needs to hear your voice,' he told me." Some delegates chuckled.

"Yeah, a bit much. But he was like that. And yeah, we had our arguments. I think we all had our arguments with him." She lowered her head for a few moments, then lifted it.

"But the things we agreed about were important. We agreed vaccine deniers are a danger to public health. We agreed that science, when applied properly, is a tool to empower all people. We also hated con artists who exploit others, and especially the poor."

"He had his flaws, and sometimes he fell short of our expectations, but he inspired so many of us. We're here now because of what he started. So can we please have a few moments of silence in his memory?"

Tom closed his eyes.

"Thank you," said Jamie. Tom opened his eyes again.

Jamie attached the mic to the stand and walked over to Pamela. They embraced.

Why did I ever think Jamie killed Reese?

***

Tom took a break from writing notes and skimmed the *Bolingbrook Star's* article on the riot. He soon wondered whether Robert himself wrote it. The piece boasted about cooperation between law enforcement agencies against "out-of-town hooligans" at a private event. Tom wondered if the *Star* rescinding their offer three years ago was for the best.

A notification popped up, announcing Trevor's latest video. Tom inserted one earpiece and played it. The video started with clips of protesters setting off fireworks, followed by clips of officers aggressively arresting them. It ended with Marty claiming the police took Meggy from her "chosen family." Tom wondered why there were no shots of her supposed kidnapping.

The video then cut to a clip recorded just after the riot. Trevor sat inside Sal's Pizza while protesters treated their wounds. One demonstrator in the background screamed as another poured bottled water on his eyes.

"Radical feminism is out of control in Bolingbrook," Trevor said solemnly. "They've imprisoned men for setting off fireworks. In the United States, we celebrate freedom with fireworks. Don't believe the lies—they assaulted us because we voiced our concern about a divisive ideology. We urge you to join us tonight outside the Bolingbrook Police Department to demand the liberation of Bolingbrook. Let the world know fireworks are free speech. Details in the description."

Tom noticed Pamela walking on stage. She whispered to the chairwoman, who nodded and approached her microphone. Tom closed his app and removed his earbud.

"We have a motion for a 30-minute recess. Is there a second?"

Several people seconded the motion. A unanimous voice vote approved it.

"Before we adjourn, I want to remind everyone to please stay inside. The protesters are gone, but law enforcement is still in the area."

Some delegates moaned. Others continued to look nervous.

"Meeting is adjourned for 30 minutes."

Tom typed a message to Trevor.

> *The fireworks were a bit much, don't you think? People could have been killed.*

Tom felt tempted to add that if their goal was to intimidate the delegates, it failed. During the morning, debate had shifted from whether to incorporate as an NPO to how to operate one. Barqah and the other Committee defectors had explained the legal issues and offered guidelines for the group. While they still had much to work on, Tom felt the delegates were moving in a common direction.

As he stood up to stretch his legs, he noticed Sakura sitting next to the jewelry booth, fidgeting with a *SheSkeptic* necklace. The vendor and a coordinator sat next to her, while other delegates stopped to greet her. Whenever anyone walked past, Sakura nodded at them without looking up, fidgeting more noticeably. Before getting caught up in the congress, Tom dismissed claims that the backlash against Sakura had traumatized her. After watching her, he regretted doubting it. He couldn't imagine what she must have gone through over the last twenty-four hours.

Tom looked down at his phone and created a new text file. Adding Sakura's perspective would strengthen both of his reports. He looked back at her and cautiously started to approach. *Don't stare. Be nice.*

"Where do you think you're going?"

Tom turned and saw Janet, the blonde coordinator, approaching.

"Well?"

Tom forced himself to smile. "I was going to introduce myself to Sakura."

"Haven't you done enough to her?" Janet positioned herself between Sakura and Tom. "You're practically president of Trevor's fan club."

Tom shook his head. "Trevor crossed the line yesterday. I'd like to tell Sakura that myself."

"I don't think she wants to see you."

Two other coordinators approached.

Tom lowered his hands. "You can accompany me if you want. Heck, I'll talk to her on stage if it makes you feel better."

She snorted. "You really don't know her, do you?"

"I'd like to."

"Mister 'facts aren't feminist' wants to know her now? Do you even read what you write?"

Pamela walked up to Janet. "What's the problem?"

"Your friend here wants to talk to Sakura."

"Okay. I'll ask if she wants to talk to Tom."

"You'll do no such thing."

Pamela raised an eyebrow. "Excuse me?"

"You know what she's been through," said Janet. "The last thing she needs is a sea lion in her face."

"Get over yourself, Janet. Starting yesterday."

"You're defending debate boy?"

"I don't want a debate," Tom protested. "I want to listen."

"Now you want to listen to her?"

Tom nodded. "Yes. Maybe I should have earlier. "

Janet snorted.

"It might help Sakura if she hears from Tom," said Pamela.

"Hear from the person who leaked her appearance here?"

More attendees focused on Tom.

"I didn't leak that. I want to hear from Sakura, not harm her. We've already lost Reese. I don't want to lose anybody else."

"Excuse me," came a steady female voice.

Tom saw Sakura coming to a stop.

"We can talk." She faced Janet. "Please."

"You don't have to—"

"I can advocate for myself," replied Sakura, louder than before. "He can speak to me. It's okay." She quickly scanned the room. "No one else needs to be removed from this congress. They win if we split." Sakura took a few breaths, glancing at Tom. "I didn't come out of hiding just to watch us scatter. I came back to help you finish what we started. Let Tom by. Please, Janet."

"You know how to reach us," Janet replied.

Sakura motioned to follow and Tom did so, keeping a respectful distance. The murmur of the delegates resumed. Weeks ago, Janet would have been right, Tom realized. He'd often imagined telling Sakura off for conspiring with

Jamie to destroy the skeptical movement. Now here she was, and he was unprepared to talk to her.

"Close the door," said Sakura as they entered the room. "Please."

Tom shut it. Behind Sakura was a long oak table, a collection of fidgets and coloring books piled at one end. Sakura leaned against a chair. Tom could see her breathing quickly.

"I'm sorry," said Tom.

"What are you sorry for?"

"For the fireworks. I've heard gunshots before. It's not like the movies." Tom fought for the words to say next. "I know I haven't—"

"Tom." Sakura lifted her arms and stared at her hands. Her breathing settled to a normal rate.

Tom slowly reached for his pocket. "May I—"

"You need to focus on the report." She lowered her hands.

"The report? You know about—"

"The Commonwealth? I know them. I've known them a long time."

As Tom stepped forward, Sakura took a step back. Embarrassed, Tom stopped in his tracks.

"Sorry." He winced. "It's been a rough few weeks for me." Tom turned red as he realized how this must sound. "I—"

"Stop." She flashed him a momentary smile, then grabbed the back of a chair and leaned on it. "I'm not one of them. If you were wondering."

Tom showed his palms. "No. No! I wasn't going to ask that." He collected himself. "I guess I need to know how we got here. What's behind all this? This congress. This rift. Is it the aliens? The Commonwealth?"

Sakura shook her head vigorously. "No. No. I understand though. When you're new, you think everything's a conspiracy. That you're just a pawn and have no control. But it doesn't work that way. There are powerful secret societies, yes, and a few are run by aliens, but most are human-led."

"Are they involved? Did they start this?"

"We started this. Skeptics. Humans. This is our doing. We made the decisions that led to this. That's why they want Jamie's report, your report, my report. They need our stories. All of them."

"I've been working on my report. Reese wanted me to. I've been taking notes—"

"That's not what they want."

Tom gave her a puzzled look.

"Think about it, Tom. Why do they need a report on this congress? They're watching us now. They know the who, what, where, when, and how." She clenched the top of the chair. "They don't know the 'why.' They don't understand why we're here—why we made the choices that led to this moment. We have to tell them why."

Tom thought for a moment. "Can't they just model our brains to find out?"

"They can't even model my brain. How can we expect them to model every human brain?"

Tom's eyes widened. "Wow. I didn't know we seemed so complicated to them."

Sakura released the chair and stepped towards Tom.

"You're new to this. New to this knowledge. New to the actual movement. Do you feel you're a pawn?"

Tom lowered his head. "Sometimes. Since Clow, it's like I'm a part of so many agendas, but I have no say in them."

"I felt that way too."

Tom lifted his head and looked at Sakura. "You do?"

"Did. Then I realized that we—humans—can decide. Each of us can decide. The scheming and conflict between the secret societies create opportunities. Look at me, Tom. Please. It takes so much for me to be here. To deal with the attacks. Losing friends. Losing my old life. But I have to give what I can. I have to save Humanist Heart, because if it dies, then Bennett and his followers win. The system wins. All the injustices will continue. And I'll live the rest of my life knowing I had the chance to fix things, but I failed."

"That's too much pressure to put on yourself. There must be other people—"

"Too many have tried! But they didn't have access to the Interstellar Commonwealth. I do. You do. We can make a difference."

Tom considered her words. "Do you want Humanist Heart to replace the Habenstein Society?"

"Not to replace. I want Humanist Heart to be another voice. A voice for change. We need to empower all people, not a select few. We need to end prejudices that divide and harm us. The Habenstein Society is right to promote science and reason, but some of their higher-ups see themselves as thought leaders. They don't question the systems of control because they want to use them. I want us to replace them."

"But replace them with what?"

"I don't know, but we have to start by asking that question. The Habenstein Society won't ask, but Humanist Heart will. The aliens can help us answer it, but we have to answer their question first."

"Which is?"

"Why? Why are we here? Why are you? That's what our reports need to say." She motioned towards the door. "I'm sorry, but I need to be alone now."

***

Tom poured a fifth packet of sugar into his cup of coffee as he watched Sakura mediate a dispute between two delegates, both of whom nodded as she talked. Tom sipped his concoction, debating if it needed more sugar. The two delegates talked to each other for several moments, then shook hands.

Sakura was the catalyst the congress had needed, thought Tom. In a matter of hours, she'd forged a consensus among the delegates, something they couldn't do in two days of debates and months of online arguments. Delegates were now using their speaking time to praise her and announce agreements. Factions that once had lists of impossible demands were compromising.

The delegates agreed to extend the last session into the evening, hoping to ratify the governing document of Humanist Heart. Watching the conversations by the stage, and coordinators furiously typing, Tom suspected the final draft was nearing completion. If they ratified it tonight, it would be because of Sakura. She looked excited, but exhausted.

Tom took another drink of his coffee and decided it did need more sugar. As he poured in his last packet, he recalled Sakura's advice. Why were they here? Had it started when he asked Jamie for coffee, or after she posted her video? Tom wondered whether the problem was more fundamental. Maybe the rifts were already present: Maybe the movement's exclusive focus on science and reason had blinded it. If so, the delegates were here because the rifts were now too wide to bridge. How did a movement dedicated to scientific skepticism come to this point?

Tom's phone vibrated. Tom pulled it out and saw a text from Trevor.

> *Isaac will explain everything tonight, including the fireworks.*

Just as Tom started typing his reply, he received a notification of a live stream from the Habenstein Society. Tom plugged in his earphones.

The stream started, and Matthew Bennett appeared, behind a desk Tom recognized as the same one Reese used for all his filmed appearances. The caption below identified Bennett as the Society's acting president.

"Good afternoon," he said. "By now you may have heard that our founder, Reese Habenstein, died yesterday. Reese was not just the father of the skeptical movement, but also a great man and a good friend. He was a giant among us, and I'm sure I speak for all skeptics when I say he will be missed. I should have details of his memorial service, and I look forward to hearing stories of how he affected our lives."

Tom shook his head and wondered if Bennett was ever friends with Reese.

The camera zoomed in.

"Before Reese died, he confided his sadness at the growing factionalism in the skeptical movement. Now I'm not a doctor, but I knew he hadn't been in the best of health lately. I think the stress from the current divide may have contributed to his decline."

He was in perfect health. He was murdered.

"I can't say for sure," Bennett went on. "But I believe the repeated allegations against a number of good men took a toll on him.

"Which brings me to the other reason for this video. I'm sure by now you've seen the violent suppression of protesters outside the Humanist Heart International congress. I may not agree with everything the protesters said, but they raise some valid questions about the direction of our movement, and they have the right to protest efforts to politicize it. Even if that involves fireworks.

"Some of today's feminists claim to be skeptics. They say their ideas belong to Western rationalism. Yesterday's violence tells us otherwise. Contemporary feminism is now divorced from rational thought. Its followers are unable to tell the difference between fireworks and gunfire. Or the difference between truth and slander.

"Now Reese was a good friend, but he thought he could bring peace between these people and rationalists. That belief cost him his life."

Tom tensed.

"As of today," said Bennett, "the Habenstein Society will stand with those who believe in free speech and equality. We will stand for free expression and oppose superstition—including politically correct superstitions."

Bennett produced a t-shirt from behind the desk and held it up to the camera. On the front were firework graphics against a black background; below were the words *FREE SPEECH*. Bennett smiled.

"Show your support for free speech and equality by buying this shirt or the cap from our website. A portion of the proceeds will go to the legal defense of wrongfully detained protesters. The rest will go towards the Society's efforts to fight dogma and honor Reese's memory. It's time to unite in his name and reject this insurgency."

Tom shook his head vigorously as Bennett went on to claim modern feminists didn't know the difference between sex and sexual assault. He remembered what Reese had told him about Humanist Heart, and about Bennett.

What his mother told him. What he'd seen during the Congress. What his father taught him.

"You're full of shit!" Tom heard himself call out. Looking up, he realized every delegate in the room was silently staring at him.

"Um," Tom struggled. "This guy." He raised his phone. "This guy is full of it—you guys are fine. I mean, everyone here. Really. Everyone here is fine. Sorry."

It seemed like the entire congress was staring at him.

"Apology accepted," the chair replied. "Please don't disturb this meeting."

Tom humbly nodded.

"Thank you. The chair recognizes the delegate."

The delegate glanced at Tom. "Someone likes us." The attendees laughed. "I move to take a 30-minute break, then let Sakura address the Congress."

"Second," Pamela yelled.

The chair called for a voice vote. No one objected.

As the chair declared the meeting adjourned, Tom stood and rushed to the Rose Garden Patio. He made his way towards the calming sounds of the fountains, leaning against the rail and watching as the water danced inside the stone-walled pools.

"Tom?" came Pamela's voice.

Tom turned towards her. "Hi."

Pamela walked up to Tom and leaned against the railing. "Are you okay?"

Tom shook his head. "I'm sorry. I was listening to someone, and... I guess it got to me."

"Who? If I can ask."

Tom pulled out his phone and showed her Bennett's video.

Pamela sighed. "I guess I shouldn't be surprised." She moved closer to Tom. "What do you think?"

Tom winced. "Once I would have supported him. But he lied in that speech. He said he was friends with Reese, but they weren't. Reese didn't want him in charge. Now I can see why. Heck, maybe all the stories about him are true." Tom sighed in frustration. "I didn't see who he was."

Pamela nodded. "There are no heroes in the movement. Even on our side of it."

"Reese will always be my hero." Tom turned back towards the fountain. "He led me this far. Now I'm lost." He looked at Pamela. "You know I didn't tell them Sakura was coming, right?"

"I know."

"Janet was going to throw me out. I wanted to listen. I tried to do everything right, but she'd made up her mind."

"She didn't throw you out, and you got to meet Sakura. She appreciated you listening."

Tom turned to Pamela. "She told you that?"

"Yes. And don't worry about Janet. She was just trying to protect Sakura."

"Protect her?"

"You're friends with Trevor, and you saw what he did."

Tom looked back at the fountains. "The fireworks were irresponsible. I shared his videos, but..." He let out a sigh and bowed his head. For a few moments, he heard only the water.

"Tom?"

"Mmm?"

"There's something I've been meaning to bring up."

"Okay."

Pamela paused. "I know you were the man in the elevator."

Tom froze in terror. For a few moments, the ground seemed to shift beneath his feet. Tom feared he might lose his balance.

Pamela continued. "I found out a while back. Jamie mentioned you might be here, and I offered to talk to you."

"She told you—"

"No!" Pamela protested. "I wanted to talk to you. I've wanted to talk to you for a long time. For so long, I wondered why the person who wrote *Skeptical Butterfly* became the one who wrote *Skeptical Hurricane*."

"Why?" said Tom as he steadied himself. "Because she hurt me. She made me out to be a monster. Or—it seemed like she said that, and it hurt. Because I just..." Tom lowered his head.

"Just what?"

"I liked her." Tom faced Pamela. "She's a brilliant singer. She was my favorite co-host. She made me laugh. And that night, I just felt as if I had one chance."

"To sleep with her?"

"No. I mean, yes. Sleep with her. But I didn't think of it that way. I just wanted some kind of connection."

"Mhmm?"

Tom gazed at the night sky.

"Bolingbrook is my home. I grew up here. But it can be a lonely place. Everyone goes to a church or a mosque. You know we have two mosques in town?" Tom closed his eyes for a moment. "Habencon was easier because most of the attendees were skeptics. But even there, part of me still held back. Part of me was afraid of being rejected. I met Matthew Bennett the last time I was there and he told me no one was off limits. I thought that meant I didn't need to be afraid, that I was holding myself back. Then when I saw Jamie walking away, it felt like I was letting my fear win. Like that was my chance to change things." Tom focused on Pamela. "I didn't want to be that shy kid again."

Pamela nodded.

"Then she made that video. She made me sound sleazy. She cost me a job. Maybe that isn't what really happened, but it seemed that way at the time. It just made me feel so angry." Tom paused. "When I criticized feminism, I gained followers. Followers who were angry too. I realized I wasn't alone. It was a kind of connection. More powerful than any connection at Habencon." He looked into Pamela's eyes. "Do you know how that feels? To know you aren't alone?"

"I do. But what did that feeling cost you?"

"A great big rift." Tom shrugged. "And losing a man I admired."

"Tom. Look at me."

Tom looked at her.

"When we were at Habencon, I had fun. I enjoyed our time together. The Tom I met was a smart, passionate person. I liked him."

"He was crushed."

"No. He was hurt and made some very poor choices. And you know, you're still that person inside. But over the years you've become so wrapped up in your own anger and pain that you can't see the truth. Maybe it feels great to have your anger affirmed, but look who's affirming it. Look at the harm they're causing. Look what they did to Sakura."

"I don't support what they did to her!"

"But you supported them overall. After all you've seen this weekend, do you still support them?"

Tom looked at the fountains, which no longer soothed him.

"Tom?"

"I don't know what to think any more. I don't know what I believe. I thought I had a clear path, but it's gone. The person who showed me the way is gone. All I know is one thing. That video. It won't go away." Tom paused. "For years I've heard the arguments against feminism. Against whisper networks. Against all this. I know there are reasons to be mad at Jamie. I know the arguments. But I don't know if they're right any more. What I thought were the facts were wrong. I need it to be rational, but maybe it's not. Maybe I've just been rationalizing it."

"Rationalizing what? The pain?"

"It has to be rational, because..."

"Because?"

"I don't know."

"Or you know the fallacy you're about to commit."

Tom chuckled. He looked at Pamela again and tried to fake a smile.

Pamela stepped away from the railing. "Tom. I can counter the arguments. I can tell you that making mistakes doesn't make you a bad person. I can tell you to move on from the pain. But I can't make you do the work. You have to pick the path forward."

"You think I know what that path is?"

"You don't. Neither do I. I wish I did. I can only imagine how unhappy the rest of your life will be. You'll keep fighting all the same battles in your head, imagining victories, but your pain will always come back. Then you'll imagine new victories. Someday you might find a way out of the whole cycle, but will you take it?" Pamela touched Tom's arm. "If you ever decide to take that path, you know where to find me."

Tom nodded and looked at the fountain as she moved her hand away.

"By the way," said Pamela. "Jamie is many things, but she's not a prize for overcoming shyness."

Tom heard Pamela walk away, followed by the patio door opening and closing. He looked up at the clear night sky. "I knew that."

No one replied.

***

Tom checked his phone. The 30 minute recess was almost over, but he felt like he'd been outside longer than that.

Tom started for the door when he heard a faint crackling hum from the direction of the practice green. He turned and made his way towards the source. Crossing the lawn, it surprised him not to see any law enforcement personnel. Had they been moved to the checkpoints?

After the practice green came into view, Tom stopped. Ahead, the generator he and Brian had worked on was now hooked up to a Tesla coil. Sparks spontaneously appeared above the coil, the hum louder at this distance. A few feet from it, Marty stood by Trevor, who was working a control panel. Noticing Tom, Marty waved both arms, then cupped his hands by his mouth. "Hey Tom," he shouted. "We called in the cavalry!"

Marty whistled, and far away, pairs of blue lights appeared in the distance, ringing the horizon within moments. Tom gasped: It was the same electric blue he saw in the rearview mirror of the Echo that night.

Before he knew it, Tom was running. Stumbling back into the lobby, he looked around, catching his breath. He still hadn't seen any law enforcement personnel.

Tom pressed into the hallway, weaving his way through the mingling delegates until he noticed Jamie entering a meeting room.

"Jamie!" yelled Tom.

Jamie didn't look at him as she closed the door.

Tom started running, bumping a few of the delegates. As he got to within a few feet of the door, a coordinator stepped into view and blocked his path. Tom stopped and caught his breath again.

"Where do you think you're going?"

Tom panted. "I need to talk to Jamie."

"She's in a meeting. And she doesn't want to speak to you."

"It's important!"

"I'm sure it is."

"No, really. We're—" Tom hesitated. How could he even begin to describe the danger? "Fine. Can you tell her it's urgent?"

"I could." He didn't move.

"Please?"

"I'll give it all the consideration you deserve."

Tom noticed Pamela approaching.

"Pamela! I need your help. I have to get a message to Jamie."

"What kind of message?"

Tom moved towards a corner and motioned for Pamela to follow.

"If you're trying to bother—"

"No!" said Tom as he stopped. Tom looked round, then whispered, "Tell Jamie we're surrounded by weredeer."

Pamela tilted her head quizzically.

"She'll know what I'm talking about. It's important. In fact, it could be the first step to fixing things." Pamela still seemed puzzled. "Please? You wanted me to choose a path forward. This is it. She'll know what I mean."

Pamela sighed. "I will."

Tom let out a sigh of relief.

"No tricks."

"Thank you!"

Pamela vanished inside the meeting room while Tom paced anxiously. Seconds later, Brian walked up to Tom and leaned over him, inches from his face. "What did I tell you?"

Tom looked at the other delegates, then turned to Brian. "Can we—"

"What were you thinking? Do you think you can just talk to her? Do you think she'll listen to you? Do you think any of them will listen?"

"We—"

"They won't. I know for a fact. They don't see you. They see someone who wronged them, and that's all. So stop—"

Brian stopped talking as the door opened. Jamie quickly walked out and approached them, her eyes locked on both men. She pivoted to Brian.

"We need to go to the Nest." She turned towards Tom. "You too."

Jamie turned and weaved through the crowd. Brian looked down at Tom, then both of them rushed to catch up with her. Once all three reached the Nest, Brian unlocked the door and turned on the overhead lights. In the center of the room, they saw a metallic arch wrapped in cables and coils. As they approached, Jamie's jaw dropped, and Tom heard static crackling around it.

"What is this?" asked Jamie.

"Whatever it is," Brian replied, "someone hooked it to the backup generator."

Jamie closed her eyes, and Tom noticed rapid movements beneath her eyelids. Jamie pivoted towards Tom and raised her right palm, then opened her eyes and stared at him.

"What is this?"

"Excuse me?"

"Don't lie to me, Tom."

"I'm not," Tom protested. "Why would you think that?"

"Because the Golf Club's advanced systems are keyed to your neural signature."

"What?"

"Don't bullshit me," snapped Jamie. "We're surrounded by weredeer, our Internet and cell phone signals are filtered, and the computer has locked out everyone except you."

The only digital equipment Tom could see was the cash register.

"All I can tell you is that I saw Trevor and Marty outside by the generator," said Tom.

"They don't have access to this kind of tech."

"Neither do I!"

"Then who?"

"I don't know," said Tom, throwing his hands up. "Maybe if you showed me this computer, I could help you."

"Help me?!"

"Yes! I know what one weredeer can do, and there's a whole army of them out there." Tom felt himself tremble. "Our feud won't matter if they slaughter us. I don't want you to die. I don't want anyone else to die." Tom glanced uneasily at the arch. "Reese was like a grandfather to us both. We were like his grandkids. He was proud of you and disappointed in me. It hurt him to see us fighting. I know he would want us to work together to save lives. So if I'm the key to unlocking the computer, tell me what to do."

Brian looked at him. "Tom—"

Jamie interrupted. "Brian, there's a direct line in Robert's office. I need you to lock yourself in. The line is blocked, but with Tom I should be able to unblock it. When you hear from me, call for help. The landlines should be the first thing I free up."

"But—"

"I need to stay here. You'll be safe in his office, and between the two of us, we should be able to put out a distress call."

Brian stared at Tom for a few moments, then unfolded his arms and walked out. Jamie watched him as he left, then turned to Tom, sighing. "If Reese were here, he would tell me you earned another second chance."

"I—"

"Prove him right."

Tom swallowed and nodded.

"The Golf Club systems are accessed through a neural network. Once you're connected, all of its systems will feel like part of you. Now close your eyes and keep them closed."

Tom did as he was told.

"While you were in a coma, they put an interface implant in your head. Imagine flipping a switch, Tom. Like you're turning on a computer in your mind."

Tom nodded as he visualized booting up his laptop.

"Okay. Now keep your eyes shut, but imagine you're opening them."

Tom remembered cartoons with point of view shots of characters opening their eyes. He imagined himself doing the same. To his surprise, a multitude of sights and sounds overwhelmed him, as if he now had more eyes and ears, each extra set connected to a different area—the kitchen, the ballroom, the Nest, the greens. Tom staggered backward and struggled to maintain his balance.

"You can filter the input. Picture yourself in a control room. Every sight is a screen. Focus on the stimuli from one screen."

Tom felt all the sensations drift away as floating screens appeared in front of him. Tom picked one, and found himself looking over the ballroom from the ceiling. The delegates were giving Sakura a standing ovation as she took to the stage. Tom could also feel the temperature of the room, and smelled the air blowing out of a nearby vent. He wondered where Pamela was, then found himself viewing the room from a different angle. In the second row, she was applauding.

"I—I'm there."

"Good. Now listen carefully to what I'm about to tell you. I need you to imagine a specific control room. The screens you visualized are on the wall of a round room. The ceiling is teal and has one recessed light. The floor is dark green. In the room are three rows of white tables. Each one has four black laptops. The login screen has a picture of Town Center."

The room materialized around Tom, followed by the laptops. Each one was equipped with a fingerprint scanner.

"I'm in. Do I touch this scanner?"

"Not yet," Jamie replied. "Imagine me there in the room."

A pirate appeared next to Tom. He recognized it as a female version of Bolingbrook High School's Raider mascot. The avatar was grayed out, like a three-dimensional image from an old TV.

"Picture me in color," the Raider told him in Jamie's voice.

The pirate transformed into a full-color avatar with vivid, realistic hues. Tom looked at himself and saw that his avatar was a male version of the mascot, also in color.

"Much better," Jamie said. She pointed at the laptop's fingerprint scanner, and Tom touched it.

The laptop and table morphed into an avatar of a gray haired man with spectacular sideburns and horn-rimmed glasses. The avatar looked at Tom, smiled, then held out its right hand. Floating text appeared between the two of them.

```
Asimov CLP. Options:
          —Run
          —Purge
          —Question
```

Tom reached for the floating menu.

"Don't touch it," said Jamie from behind him. Tom turned and saw her sitting behind a laptop in the next row.

"What is it?"

"It's an AI that's attuned to you. Whoever put it here gave it access to the entire operating system. They also set it up so you're the only one who can run it."

"What does it do?"

```
Information not found. Options:
               —Run
               —Purge
               —Question
```

Tom looked at Jamie.

"Since you upped my clearance level, I should be able to figure something out."

Tom then heard someone laughing in the real world. Instinctively, he shifted his perceptions back to his body. By the main door of the Nest, he saw Brian standing next to Marty, who held the door for Trevor.

"Brian?" asked Jamie. "What are you doing?"

"They know how to treat their allies," said Brian coldly. "Unlike you."

Chapter 10

*"The crusader, the jihadist, and the eugeni-
cist may have different motivations, but that
matters very little to their victims."*
—Sakura Takahashi, "Not All Sides"

TREVOR WHEELED PAST BRIAN to park himself by the
arch. "Is he ready?"

"She taught him already," said Brian, glancing at Jamie.
"Saved me a job."

Jamie glared back. "Tell me you're not working with
these MRA clowns."

Brian shrugged. "I got tired of all the rejections. Trevor
and I may have our disagreements, but he appreciates me."

"You sick fuck. And I guess whoever's behind all this
appreciates you?"

"Behind this?"

"Come on. We both know these two don't have the
brains to source this kind of tech."

"You might be surprised," replied Trevor with a smirk, not looking up from his tablet.

"Isaac," said Tom, causing everyone else to look at him. "He's behind this. That's why the AI looks like Isaac Asimov. He gave you this tech, didn't he?"

Marty and Brian turned towards Trevor.

"You'll excuse me if I'm a bit busy," he muttered, still focused on the tablet. "A rift is just about to form. The equipment you assembled for us allows us to move it here and counter the temporal skip."

"So Isaac *is* behind this. Wait—he's the time traveler?"

"He's *a* time traveler."

Tom approached Trevor until Brian stepped in front of him. As Trevor quickened his keystrokes, visible currents flowed through the coils and electrical bolts filled the archway.

"You might want to move back," Trevor told Tom. He nodded at Jamie. "She can do whatever she wants."

Tom and Jamie each took a few steps away from the arch. The metal frame glowed red, and Tom could feel the heat from where he stood. Moments later, the bolts of electricity started moving erratically, like a video being sped up and rewound. The space within the archway turned pitch black, and the hum grew so loud that Tom almost covered his ears. Bright lights erupted from the archway, blinding him. Moments later, the spots in his vision cleared and the room cooled.

Tom struggled to understand what he now saw within the archway. It was as if the fabric of reality was parting like a curtain, revealing a room. Two figures stood there, both in black full-body suits. Tom recognized one as the intruder from the hotel, while the other was taller, even while hunched over a console. Behind them, a generator was shooting sparks. The taller traveler stood and turned to face Tom, who felt himself being stared at.

"Tom," said the man, whose voice sounded to Tom like a computer attempting to sound British. "So good to finally see you. I planned for everything, except how I'd feel."

Tom and the traveler looked at each other for several moments.

"You're Isaac," Tom finally said.

The traveler nodded. "You've called me Isaac. I think you know where I got the name. Isaac Asimov—among history's greatest writers and the twentieth century's most visionary minds. Zipped by ivory tower feminists."

"You should have gone back further in time," said Jamie. "Then you'd realize his so-called vision was about finding asses to grope."

"Jamie Kyle," said the traveler. "SheSkeptic. Feminist. Cosmic pop star. *Shut up.*" He turned to Tom. "You don't know what it means to tell her that. To finally face her and have a winning plan."

"Did your plan involve killing Reese?" Tom asked, struggling to keep his voice from breaking.

"I'm sorry you saw that," the traveler replied. "But he needed to die."

Jamie's jaw dropped. "You murdered Reese?"

"I put him down," the other traveler replied calmly, speaking for the first time.

"Put him *down*?" asked Jamie. "Reese wasn't a sick animal. He was a human being. A loving human being, and you killed him. Both of you killed him. You're worse than they are." She nodded towards Marty and Trevor. "You're an insult to everything Asimov claimed to be."

Marty started towards Jamie, who span to face him, locking her eyes on his. "Try it and you'll regret it." Marty blinked, then stopped in his tracks.

"Jamie's right." All eyes turned to Tom again. "Both of you murdered Reese." Tom glared at the first traveler and stepped towards the rift, static crackling between them. "Why?"

"To fix the past," said the second traveler.

"More than that," said the first. "To save humanity. Because that old fool wouldn't get out of the way, when he finally died and I got the Society, it was too late." He motioned at Jamie. "That lying cunt was already too powerful."

"Not powerful enough if you're here," Jamie replied.

"Always with the comebacks," snapped the first traveler. "Never an apology. Never willing to compromise. Always against me."

"Why?" asked Tom. "Why couldn't you work it out with her?"

"Why? Have you forgotten what she did to you? I had to save the movement from her."

"Or was she stopping you from taking over the movement?" asked Tom. "Was that your real plan... Dr. Bennett?"

The traveler moved his head back, then laughed. "Bennett? That over-educated fool nearly annihilated Earth. I stopped him. I saved humanity. Then she turned everyone against me, again. I—" The traveler's voice became garbled, like a lagging internet stream.

"Again?" asked Jamie. "Who the fuck are you?"

"Let me show you," replied the traveler, now speaking with a purely digital voice. He started unhooking the mask from his suit.

"No!" yelled the second traveler, who grabbed his arm.

"It's all right," reassured the first. He touched her hand. "They have to see." Though the voice was digital, Tom heard sadness in its tone.

The second traveler held the first's hand for a moment, then stepped away. As the first shed his mask, Tom gasped. He was looking at a man in his early forties, old burn scars lining his neck and face, the blood vessels in his eyes glowing blue. It was an older man, but his features were unmistakably familiar.

"You had a crush on Cassie in middle school," said the traveler, who both sounded and looked like Tom. "You wanted to write a newsletter under the pseudonym Anteros. The password for the Box of Adventure was anti-rock. You thought about buying a gun before interviewing the student president at UIC. Is that enough, or do I need to mention that special game you and Ashley played?"

Tom swallowed. "You're from the future." There were other possibilities, he thought, but amazingly, this was the most probable.

"Good," replied the traveler. "Because I've worked hard to get back to this point." He sighed. "You look so young. I still remember all the pain. You think it's bad, but it gets so much worse. No matter what I accomplished, I couldn't make it go away." He turned to face Jamie. "I wish I could make you feel a fraction of what you inflicted."

"I'm fine."

"When we're done, you won't be."

"What do you mean?" asked Tom.

The traveler kept his eyes on Jamie. "Any snappy comeback you want to add?"

"Don't let me interrupt your reunion."

"What do you mean?" Tom insisted.

"I mean we're about to extract a cancer from the skeptical movement." The traveler faced Tom and grinned. "The bomb. The right emails. The weredeer. All part of a plan to purge our movement of feminists, and save humanity."

"When did you become Hari Seldon?" Jamie asked, glancing between both Toms.

The traveler turned towards Trevor's group. "Brian. Marty. It's time."

Brian nodded and made his way towards the door. Marty followed.

"Wait," said Trevor, making eye contact with Marty. "I may have been hard on you, but you needed it. I never questioned your enthusiasm, but I questioned your maturity." Marty frowned as he looked down at Trevor. "Not any more. You've earned your place in history. Now go make it."

The traveler nodded.

Marty grinned at Jamie. "You're gonna be infamous when we're done."

"It's where you wanted it," Brian told Trevor. He and Marty left the Nest.

The traveler turned his attention back to Tom. "You met the Asimov AI. Your job is to run it. Right now, all Humanist Heart's figureheads are in one place. Our allies have taken care of the police. The Golf Club's defenses are deactivated."

"Damn it," said Jamie, finally sounding fearful. "He's right."

"When you activate Asimov, Marty and Brian will enter the ballroom and open fire on the delegates."

"Motherfucker!" yelled Jamie, making for the door.

"I wouldn't do that," said Trevor. Jamie spun to face him. Trevor reached under the table and pulled out a pistol, pointing it at Jamie. He motioned with the gun for her to move closer to Tom. Jamie complied.

"Mass murder?" asked Tom. "That's what this is all about?"

"It's more than that. It's a chance to build a new world. We'll pull humanity out of the dark age of irrationality and secure its place in the Interstellar Commonwealth. It'll be the start of a new enlightenment, guided by great men. I've done my part. Now it's up to you."

"This is your chance to fix the past," added the second traveler. "Instead of being the villain, you'll be the hero."

"Yes," said the first. "After the shooting, Asimov will alter all video footage to show Jamie shooting first."

"With the delegates caught in the crossfire," Trevor calmly added. He smirked at Jamie. "Fortunately, Tom will intervene. He'll be the brave hero, and you'll be the monster."

"It won't work," said Jamie. "There will be hundreds of eyewitnesses."

"Eyewitnesses?" the traveler snorted. "Asimov's alterations will be undetectable. It won't matter how many eyewitnesses defend you. When the video gets released, the world will believe it."

"Your case will become a textbook example of feminist false accusations," Trevor added.

"So that's your plan," said Jamie. "A mass gaslighting event."

The traveler chuckled. "I prefer to think of it as a hoax."

"A hoax?"

"In a sense," said the traveler. "Just like Reese used hoaxes to reveal greater truths, I'll reveal your nature to the world. You're a monster, Jamie. A monster who devours innocent people. You said I threatened you in that elevator. Your video spread so far and got viewed so many times that it became the truth. Now I'll destroy you with a video, just as you tried to destroy me."

"You're making a pretty damn good argument for destroying you. You're not rationalists, you're murderers!"

"And you're a slander merchant," said the traveler.

"It wasn't slander," Tom replied. Both Jamie and the traveler looked at him as if taken by surprise. "Jamie was telling the truth from her perspective. She isn't trying to destroy the movement. Reese even approved of her working with Humanist Heart."

"That's why he had to die!" the traveler shot back. "All those years he spent apologizing for that monster. Run Asimov and you can change the world! Feminism, religion, social justice crap. All the superstitions will fall. The Commonwealth will accept humanity, and you'll be remembered among history's great men."

"Bullshit!" yelled Jamie. "Tom, listen to me. I've traveled across the entire galaxy. I've met the Commonwealth's leaders. They share Humanist Heart's values. You do this, and they'll finally give up on us."

"*Liar*," the traveler spat back. "The last time they almost abandoned us, it was because of cranks like you!" Tom remembered what Reese had told him about the sixties. "Consider this," the traveler added. "If I'm wrong, why hasn't the Commonwealth stopped us? We all know they're watching right now."

Tom looked up at the ceiling, then back at the traveler. "Why can't you run Asimov? Why do I need to do it?"

"The temporal erosion caused by Reese's death almost destroyed our reactor," the traveler replied. "Just keeping the rift open uses most of our power. If either of us passed through now, the crossing would kill us. It has to be you, Tom."

"And if I refuse?" The travelers looked at each other.

"Then you'll have a bigger problem," Trevor replied. "Look outside." Via his implant, Tom gazed out from the roof of the clubhouse. The fiery blue glow of weredeer eyes surrounded him on all sides. "That's my family."

"Family?" Tom asked.

"Yes. My father is the leader of the Free Roamers. What humans would call feral weredeer. Right now they're waiting on you, Tom. If you don't run Asimov, they'll attack. Even if you reactivate your defenses, we'll get past them. Then they'll slaughter every human they see. You, Jamie, Brian, Marty, Sakura, or me. It won't matter to them."

"No," said Jamie.

"Then they'll keep going. They'll roll through Bolingbrook and kill the weredeer who refused to join my father. Then they'll kill everybody else. Your classmates, your neighbors, your family. Everybody in Bolingbrook."

"You genocidal dumbass!" yelled Jamie.

"Think of it as a trolley problem," said the traveler. "The simplest trolley problem ever. Save humanity. Save yourself. It's the right choice. Run the program, or thousands die because of your indecision. We are humanists. We know what the right decision is."

"You think mass murder is humanist?" said Jamie.

"If it's for the good of humanity, then yes."

"Wait," said the second traveler, as Jamie looked sickened, then stepped towards the rift. Sparks rained as she removed her mask. Tom didn't recognize her burn-marked face, but he recognized her smile.

"Meggy?"

"Megan," she corrected. "I've always wanted to see this version of you."

"You murdered Reese?"

"To save us. I know your pain, Tom. When I met you, I was lost and frightened. Marty did me so much damage. He went out of his way to make me feel worthless. I can't forget all the ways he hurt me. And nobody helped me."

"I'm so sorry."

Megan looked at Tom and smiled. "I remember when you said that to me after I dropped out of high school. We didn't know it at the time, but that was our first date."

"Jesus," Jamie told the traveler. "You're a groomer and a murderer."

"So typical of you to see me as a victim," Megan laughed. "Because that's how you see yourself. I was the one who pursued Tom." Jamie looked back, clenching her jaw, as Megan turned back to him. "I was broken when we met. Once Marty started telling me to kill myself, I thought if I pretended to love you, I could get free.

"I went through the motions. I pretended. Then one night, you showed me Embassy Row. You told me about what Jamie did—how it nearly destroyed you. I know what it's like when someone exploits your affections—the pain you feel when somebody you trust vandalizes your heart. At some point, I realized I wasn't just pretending anymore.

"You'll never know how much I wished I could heal you—wished I could take away all of the pain. When I found out about the plan, I felt so happy I could finally save you. Save myself. Save the world."

"By becoming an assassin?" replied Jamie.

"I did what needed to be done." Tom shifted as Megan faced him. "One way or another, Marty and I both meet our ends tonight. I have nothing to lose, but the me in your time has everything to gain. She'll be free, Tom. Help her like you helped me. Lift her up. Show her she has a future. You can guide her down a new path. Run Asimov, and you'll save both of us."

Both Megan and the traveler looked back at Tom expectantly.

"Do you remember Pamela?" he asked.

"Who?" said the traveler.

Tom blinked. He couldn't imagine himself forgetting Pamela.

"This is what matters, Tom. You know I'm right. It's a simple trolley car problem with a simple solution."

"You can do it," Megan added. "You can save both of us."

"Feminism or your family, Tom," said Trevor with a sigh, his gun still trained on them. "That's your choice, and you're running out of time."

As Trevor, Jamie, and the traveler started talking at once, Tom shifted his focus to the control room in his mind, muting sounds from the Nest. The Asimov AI noticed him and approached.

"What would the real Isaac Asimov do?" Tom asked.

```
Asimov CLP. Options:
      —Run
      —Purge
    —Question
```

"Never mind," Tom grumbled.

The traveler's words haunted him. Why, he wondered, wasn't the Commonwealth intervening? They could stop all this if they wanted to. Tom remembered Sakura telling him the Commonwealth wanted to know why all of this was happening. If so, he thought, maybe their inaction wasn't a sign of approval, but that they were still observing. Maybe, Tom decided, it was time to turn the question around. Why did the Commonwealth still care about humanity?

In the fifties, Reese had told him, the Commonwealth were almost ready to reveal themselves, but the rise of pseudoscience in the sixties had all but compelled them to give up hope. He recalled the technological advances that followed World War Two. If the Commonwealth only cared about science, he could understand why they balked at what came next. But organized skepticism had only started in the seventies. What had kept them on board till then?

"If there could be a civil rights movement, and a women's movement," Reese had told him at Clow, "why not a skeptical movement?" Of course, Tom thought: *social progress*. Desegregation. Decolonization. Democratic uprisings. Voting rights. Women's rights. If the Commonwealth shared Humanist Heart's values, they must have approved of all this. Tom shook his virtual head for not thinking of it sooner.

Focus on the question of why, he told himself, thinking of Sakura. Maybe, he thought, the Commonwealth wanted to know if humans could achieve both scientific and social progress—whether the skeptical movement could figure out how to combine the two.

Tom looked back at the Asimov AI.

```
Asimov CLP. Options:
    -Run
    -Purge
    -Question
```

"Your books made it seem so easy," he said, then glanced at the virtual ceiling again. "This might not be the answer you want, but you should listen to it."

Tom shifted his mind back to his body. "I've made a decision," he said, causing the others in the Nest to fall silent. "You're right—this is a trolley car problem. A simple one. But you? You have a much bigger problem."

"What problem?" asked the traveler.

Tom felt a chill as he looked into his future self's eyes. "I figured out what all this really is. This isn't some noble crusade against feminism or the forces of superstition or even Jamie. It's simpler than that. This is about your inability to accept rejection." Tom shook his head as the traveler tensed. "Jamie doesn't think of herself as a victim. You do."

"How can you say that?"

"You think of me as a younger you. I'm not. The moment you entered the past, you caused more changes than you anticipated. Because of you, I came here and met Pamela again. She's a much better humanist than either you or me. She reminded me of what humanism really is. This? This isn't humanism. This is your rage. This is you lashing out no matter who it harms. Your obsession has consumed and corrupted you."

Megan stepped closer to the rift. "You don't know what you're saying. You need to run Asimov. There's so much you don't know about our time. About how much worse things get."

"But your time doesn't exist any more. I've met the younger you—that means we're both on a new path! If your goal was to change the past, you succeeded. You don't need to keep killing. It's over. You've won."

Megan stared back at Tom, seemingly unable to speak or look away.

"Irrelevant!" the traveler replied. "This is the plan. You know what happens if you don't run Asimov. Your inaction will kill thousands!"

"Not my inaction. Your actions." Tom faced Megan. "Right now, that weredeer army is the biggest threat to your younger self. If either one of you don't call them off, she and thousands of others will be killed—because of you. Either one of you can end this. Let them live. Let us live."

"That's headless humanist crap!" the traveler yelled.

"Then I would rather die," retorted Tom, "than be a heartless humanist!" He closed his eyes. "What happens next is up to you. Asimov. Purge."

As Tom opened his eyes, Trevor and Megan stared at him in disbelief. The traveler slowly moved away from the rift towards Megan. "He should have said yes. I would have said yes."

Megan glanced at Tom, then looked at her companion. She smiled at him. "We've won."

"What?"

"He's not you anymore." She held out her hands.

The traveler intently stared at Tom for a few moments, then took Megan's hands. "This is what you want?" She nodded. The traveler turned to Trevor. "Call them off."

"Excuse me?"

"I said call them off. It's over."

With his free hand, Trevor began tapping his tablet's screen. "Sorry. I'm sticking to the plan."

"You might want to listen to him," Jamie advised.

Trevor smirked. "Why would I do that?"

"While you guys were talking about trolley cars and humanism, I found a backdoor in your program and sent a distress signal."

"Impossible," replied the traveler.

"Hey. Crappy code is crappy code, even if it's from the future." She grinned at Trevor. "Might want to tell your army to head on home."

"Oh they'll go home," said Trevor. "After mauling every headless humanist here. I just hope I live to see it." Trevor tapped the tablet. "Do it," he spoke into the microphone, then smiled at Jamie. "The cavalry is on its way."

"Can't wait."

Tom's skin tingled as he sensed Jamie taking control of the Nest. The televisions powered on, showing hundreds of weredeer charging at the clubhouse. Through his implant, Tom felt the ground vibrate.

"I failed you," the traveler told Megan as fires broke out from their generator.

Trevor calmly focused on the screens showing the weredeer.

Moments later, several glowing saucer shaped vessels appeared above the clubhouse—Tom recognized them from the *Babbler* as Torresian battleships. Each emitted what looked like a spotlight, and the weredeer caught in it galloped slowly into the air, like reindeer in a stop-motion holiday special. The weredeer kicked and slashed in vain as the saucers swallowed them, while those not caught in the beams fled, pursued by other ships.

Trevor tapped his tablet. "Go. Change of plans. Do it. Take out as many as you can." He looked at Jamie. "I know how to improvise."

"And I have my own cavalry."

The televisions switched to show Brian and Marty marching towards the ballroom, where Tom sensed all staff and delegates were. Suddenly, he felt others with them in the corridor. On the screens, Brian and Marty stopped in their tracks, Marty pointing his gun in all directions. Brian remained motionless.

"You don't scare me," said Marty, failing to sound intimidating. He fired two shots in one direction, then two in another. Six men in blue walked into view, and Marty backed away towards Brian.

"Brian? I need to know what to aim for. The head? The chest? I can't go down like this—Brian!"

Brian stood still, while the gun in his hand visibly shook. The men in blue closed in, and Brian placed his gun in his own mouth as Marty called his name. The screens blinked off, but Tom heard the gunshot before the audio cut out.

Jamie shook her head with a sigh. "I wish he'd surrendered. At least the sound dampeners worked. Sakura's on fire tonight."

On the other side of the rift, alarms sounded. After the traveler deactivated them, Megan rushed to operate another control panel.

Trevor lowered his head and shook it, then looked up at Tom. "I forgive you." He looked at Jaime. "You do what you do because you're a cunt. Now you'll have to live with that." Trevor tapped on his tablet, then tossed it away. Outside, Tom could now hear the rising hum of the generator, which sounded like it was about to overload. Trevor moved back towards the table, then looked at the travelers.

"Save humanity. Destroy feminism. I gave up everything for your plan. All you both had to do was stick to it."

"It won't matter soon," said the traveler.

"But in the meantime, it matters to me." Before anyone could react, Trevor turned his gun on the traveler, firing shot after shot. The traveler's suit rippled as the bullets hit; he staggered back, only to be struck by an arc from the generator. The traveler began to convulse as he collapsed. When his gun clicked emptily, Trevor tossed it aside to glare at Megan. "Any last words?"

Megan faced Tom. "If you see Meggy, tell her about the great lake." Tom nodded in recognition. "Tell her she's not a fool. Tell her she can slay a dragon." As Trevor watched, Megan pulled out the same sharp object Tom had seen at the hotel.

"Even in this chair, you still can't beat me."

"I know."

Trevor charged at Megan. Static sparked from his wheelchair, but Trevor kept spinning the wheels. As Trevor crossed the rift, Megan threw the object at the generator, which promptly exploded. Less than a second later, a shockwave knocked Tom to the ground, upending nearby chairs and tables. Behind him, he heard the windows shatter, followed by the sound of blast shields hitting the floor. As the rift closed, sparks rained down from the arch. Moments later, it powered down, and Tom heard the muffled sound of an explosion outside. Tom sat up, gazed at where the rift had been, felt himself trembling, then dropped to the ground and started crying.

"You know," said Jamie, looking down at him. "I sure could use a goddamn cup of coffee now."

***

Tom sipped his sugar-filled coffee, then set his cup back down. Jamie sat at an adjacent table, finishing hers reluctantly. Beyond the blast shields, Tom sensed the cleanup crews stealthily restoring the club grounds to normal. In the ballroom, Pamela moved for a vote to approve incorporation papers for a Humanist Heart non-profit. Delegates unanimously approved.

"That's bound to make the Commonwealth happy," said Jamie, breaking the silence. "They'll make a large donation to Humanist Heart once they're set up. The Habenstein Society will get a smaller donation. Bennett won't be happy, but I couldn't give a fuck about him."

Tom took another sip.

"Robert's gonna be down here soon," said Jamie. "He's still overseeing the clean-up outside."

Tom nodded. "Was I right about them changing things? Am I still on the path that leads to... that?"

"It's up to you. You've been given a rare opportunity to change your future. Just don't expect another chance. You're not that privileged."

Tom chuckled, then took in the wreckage around them.

"They used to have good instant coffee here," remarked Jamie. "This tastes like piss. I should have fired up the espresso machine."

Tom set his cup aside. "Jamie," he began. "I don't know the right way to say this."

"Just say it. I'm not in the mood for pleasantries."

Tom considered his words. "At Habencon, I slept with a few attendees. Consensually, of course."

"I'd hope so."

Tom nodded. "I should go further back. I'm from a liberal family. My parents raised me as a feminist. So when I saw your video..."

Tom felt Jamie's critical gaze on him.

"The main thing is, while I was drunk, that doesn't excuse me for acting like a jerk. I didn't mean to treat you like a conquest, but I did. You're funny, brilliant, and talented. Humanity's best musical ambassador. You weren't my prize for being courageous. I understand that now."

"Are you trying to flatter me?"

"No. I'm saying you didn't deserve how I treated you that night. You were tired, and I ignored your wishes. I was a stranger hitting on you, and you had every right to feel uncomfortable."

"Especially in an elevator."

Tom winced. "You're right. When I saw your video, I..." He looked around, trying to think of what to say. "I was too arrogant to listen to what you actually said. I was hurt, but it wasn't you that upset me. It was the thought that I didn't live up to my ideas. I didn't want to face that, so

I turned to people who made me feel good about myself. I rationalized my actions and made things worse. I unleashed so much harm because I didn't want to face the truth."

He looked at Jamie, who kept her critical gaze on him.

Tom took another breath. "I'm sorry I made you uncomfortable in that elevator. No—what I mean is, I'm sorry I was a selfish jerk that night. And I'm sorry I contributed to the years of hate and misinformation you've faced. I failed as a skeptic, and you suffered. I'm... I'm sorry." Tom shrugged. "I'm just sorry."

Jamie silently considered Tom's words. "First off. You were a fucking jerk that night. Then you kept being a fucking jerk all these years."

Tom nodded shamefully.

"You helped inspire MRAs to riot against us. We had to rely on the police to protect us. Do you know how many people here have been traumatized by police? The Bolingbrook cops aren't as bad as the Chicago cops, but they can still be pretty fucking bad. Robert was trying to impress the Commonwealth. If we'd held the congress elsewhere, who knows what might have happened? And let's not forget that a couple of nights ago, you were an *asshole* to me at the hotel. I wasn't sure if you were going to assault me."

Tom shook his head.

"Do you know how many times I've been told to forgive you? Do you know how painful it was to hear Reese come up with excuse after excuse? Saying sorry isn't enough—you need to change. You need to stop being an asshole and knock off your 'modern feminism' act. Feminism is not woo, Tom, and it's not just about women. Because I don't have to forgive you because you're sorry. I'll forgive you when you've earned my forgiveness. If you can't earn it, then stay the hell out of my way."

Tom fidgeted.

Jamie paused for several moments. "I can't help you," she added finally. "But Pamela is willing to."

"Okay."

"And as for being a terrible skeptic, let me say this. Accepting you made a mistake and owning up to that makes you a better skeptic than most leaders of the Habenstein Society."

Tom bit his lip as Jamie continued. "I accept your apology, but you still have to earn my forgiveness."

"Agreed."

Jamie held out her hand. Tom firmly shook it, before their phones buzzed at the same time. Tom picked his up and saw a text from an unknown number.

> `Thank you for your report.`

Jamie put down her phone. "I guess we won't be writing those tonight."

"I guess not," Tom said with a smile. "One less worry."

Another text message appeared, but this one seemed to float in front of Tom.

> `I'm coming down. BBMayor`

"He won't be happy," sighed Tom.

"I know." Jamie stood. "One last thing: I've performed here many times and I know Robert fairly well. He'll probably offer you a job. Now, he can be a real hardass, but if you get on his good side, he can be a first-rate teacher. Something to think about."

"I will."

Jamie nodded, then walked away. Tom felt a wave of serenity wash over him as he let go of his rage.

Tom heard movement in the hallway. Using the implant, he saw three men in blue approaching, two of them dragging Marty by the arms. Tom switched his senses back to his body. The first man in blue opened the door, then held it as the other two dragged Marty inside and dropped him to his knees. Marty's head swayed as he opened his eyes.

Robert walked in and looked at Tom. "I've seen the log. Anything you want to add, Tom?"

"I didn't know about the plan," Tom replied. "If I had, I'd have warned you."

Robert nodded. He walked up to Marty and peered down at him.

"You've been a very naughty resident. Thought martyrdom could redeem you?"

"Fuck off."

Robert smirked. "I'm the mayor of Bolingbrook. I'm the one who tells people to fuck off."

Marty unconvincingly pretended to laugh. He looked at the men holding him down, then back at Robert. "How could you side with them? I thought you believed in traditional values."

"I'm asking the questions, not you. Who helped you? Brian couldn't have done this alone. Who was he working for?" Robert stood up. "I'm still in a good mood, so if you tell me now, you can still come out of this as a functioning adult."

"Tell me why you betrayed the men of Bolingbrook, and I might forgive you."

Tom tried to speak, but Robert raised his hand.

Marty continued. "Go ahead. You don't know what you're up against. I'm one soldier in an army of men. They'll come for me, and when the men of Bolingbrook see an army fighting for them, they'll join our side, while you'll be tossed out with the garbage. Bolingbrook belongs to men like me, not appeasers like you."

Robert looked down at Marty and shook his head. Marty laughed.

"Let me make this clear," said Robert. "I've been the mayor of Bolingbrook for over thirty years. I've always helped men. Before you were born, I was bringing good paying jobs to Bolingbrook. While you were still flunking toilet training, I added more housing subdivisions. While you were ruining your mother's relationships, I was packing the school board. All those things helped the men in our community. And let's not forget that when you endangered all the men in Bolingbrook today, I was busting my ass to keep them safe."

Robert crouched down and locked eyes with Marty.

"You've never fought for men. Your so-called movement is a lie. I don't see you fighting for men. I see you threatening women. That's not being a man. That's being a bully, and I've faced down bullies far, far stronger than you. They're the ones who end up in the garbage."

Marty glared at Robert. "You'll change your tune when cunts and freaks overrun Bolingbrook."

"I doubt it. Because I don't care what Bolingbrook looks like. Just as long as I stay in charge."

Robert nodded at the third man in blue, who slapped Marty. Marty slumped over and Robert lifted his chin.

"Strength is about more than muscles or the size of your dick." Robert turned to the man in blue. "Clean out his memories from middle school on. Leave that part in."

Robert stood up and approached Tom. "I think a decade or two on Pluto will set him straight. He'll learn what a real matriarchy is like." Robert walked up to the blast shields, which retracted. He watched as the repair crew finished filling in the crater where the generator used to be.

"Here's your first village skeptic assignment. We need a cover story. I'll give you the main outline. We'll say the UFOs were drones and blame one of the Douglas kids. That family's been a pain in my ass for years. We'll say Trevor and Marty ran off with the donations they raised. I have friends in the Bahamas who can share pictures of them on the beach. It might be fun to send their friends on a global goose chase." He chuckled. "As for Brian, suicide works. We can fake some gambling debts, and say he tried to swipe money from the cash register. When confronted, he killed himself. Are you taking this down?"

"No," Tom replied.

"No?" Robert asked, still surveying events outside.

"No. I don't work for you. Robert, my name is Tom Larsen, and I'm a freelance reporter for the *Bolingbrook Babbler.*" Tom pulled out his cell phone and activated the recording app. "Mayor Robert Clark, a weredeer army recruited by a time traveler almost stormed Bolingbrook. Do you have a comment?"

One man in blue turned to face Tom.

Tom acknowledged the man, then focused on Robert. "Can you tell me which staff members you suspect—"

Robert continued to look outside as he interrupted. "I can make it look like you tried to kill yourself by inhaling car exhaust through a hose. Only you passed out and ended up—"

"No. You won't."

Robert turned towards Tom.

"Your greatest achievements are classified, and I know that bothers you. You let the *Babbler* publish their stories because you hope that someone will read them and believe the truth about you. Even if it's just one person. Even if that one person is a kid in a supermarket. It means someone will know you're the most important mayor in the galaxy. You won't pass up this opportunity to tell your side of the story."

Tom marched up to Robert and held the phone up to his face. "A weredeer army just tried to attack Bolingbrook. Do you have a comment for that kid?"

Robert gave a nod to the man in blue. Abruptly, Tom felt intense pain in his left ear. As he dropped to his knees, he felt a warm liquid running down the side of his neck, and something drilling its way through his ear canal. Tom screamed as he felt his nerves tear, his senses shutting down one at a time. He collapsed to the floor as the pain overwhelmed him. As it subsided, something crawled out of his ear. No longer in pain, Tom reached for and reluctantly looked at the object. It was a tiny black cylinder covered in blood and clear ooze.

A man in blue held out his hand. After taking a moment, Tom put the object on the man's palm. The man took it and moved away.

Robert approached, holding Tom's phone up to his face, and spoke. "Don't settle for being a nice guy. Strive to be a great man."

Robert lowered the phone, then tapped the screen. He leaned over to return it to Tom, who gently took it back.

"That's my quote for today, Tom. Goodbye."

Epilogue

"Hurricanes may or may not result from distant butterflies flapping their wings. Either way, the result is an indiscriminately destructive storm. Unlike a butterfly, I know my actions have consequences. Effective today, I am shutting down Skeptical Hurricane, *and leaving the movement. You don't have to join me, but if you stay, I ask that you practice skepticism as well as preaching it."*
—Tom Larsen, "What I learned from getting stuck in an elevator"

TOM WALKED TOWARDS HIS father's shop, sifting through keys in one hand and fumbling with his phone in the other. Working a weekend afternoon wasn't his idea of fun, but his dad had asked him to mind the store, adding that something had come up. After the week they'd had since Tom's story broke in the *Babbler*, he wasn't about to argue—and after everything he'd been through, he needed a break.

On his phone, Tom launched the app for the store's alarm system. To his surprise, it hadn't been activated. Seeing no sign of a break-in, he assumed his dad must have forgotten to turn it on when he locked up. *Not like him*, Tom thought with a shrug.

As he unlocked the store, turning the door sign to *Open*, Tom heard movement from the backroom. "Hello?" he asked, suddenly wondering if he should be running.

"Tom?" came a voice.

Tom cautiously approached the door to the backroom. Peeking inside, he discovered Meggy behind his father's desk. She slid off the chair and rushed towards him.

"Meggy? What are you doing here?"

"Waiting for you. I have a surprise." She reached for Tom's hand and tugged. He followed her back to the desk, where she opened a blue notebook with yellow stars on the cover. The first page had a drawing of Meggy and Tom as astronauts, planting a flag on a rocky surface. "We're on the moon!"

"Wait! How did you get in here?"

"I walked in."

Tom stared back, dumbfounded. "You just walked in?"

"I asked if I could see you," said Meggy, eyes bright with excitement. "Your dad said you were out, and I was too young to play with you. Then he told me to go home. But this place is so neat..."

"So you stayed put?"

"I opened the door and acted like I was walking out. Then he got a phone call. When he looked away, I let the door close and hid."

"He didn't see you?"

Meggy grinned. "I was quiet."

"What about the alarm?"

"I waited until he stepped out and locked the door. Then I pressed the cancel button and came back here. I even drew more pictures."

Tom blinked. "You came here to show me pictures?"

"Kinda." Meggy picked up her tablet from the desk. "I need your help. I couldn't write you because my tablet is sick."

"Sick? How?" Meggy bowed her head and Tom sighed. "You can tell me. I won't get mad." Meggy slowly looked up at Tom.

"Marty never came home from the big fight. Mom says it's because he grew up and went away. Now Dad is coming over more. He even took me to the Museum of Science and Industry."

"The best museum ever! I like him."

Meggy giggled. "It's different when he's around. I think he's moving back in." She fidgeted for a moment. "I sorta want him to." Tom nodded. "But I think I messed it up."

"How?"

"Marty's friends. They broke my tablet. Then told Mom and me the police couldn't protect us."

"That's terrible. You and your mom don't deserve that. I thought they were my friends too. Then I realized who they really are."

"They lied. They said I was special, but they knew I was dumb."

Meggy started crying, then tightly embraced Tom. As he comforted her, he noticed his Ethical Sunday School drawings, now framed and hanging by his father's monitor. Tom remembered feeling embarrassed when his dad first hung them there, saying he wanted a reminder of why he started the shop. Meggy released Tom, who found a cloth on the desk and handed it to her, before noticing her tablet. "Let me see if I can fix that."

As Meggy wiped her eyes, Tom booted up the desktop and connected the tablet. "Let me tell you a story while we wait,' he said, removing the relevant drawings from the wall and placing them along the desk. "I drew these when I was about your age. They tell a story from my Sunday school." He started running an anti-malware program, and motioned at the faded image of a dragon atop a pile of rulebooks. "A long time ago, there was a young stable girl who was brought to a dragon's lair. His name was Dogma, the dragon of rules."

"He looks scary."

"He was, and the girl was frightened. But she was also parched with thirst. So she asked for a small cup of water."

"What did he say?"

"Dogma roared at the girl, picked up a stone, and handed it to her, telling her to squeeze water out of it." Tom saw a stress ball with a CAS logo on it, and handed it to Meggy, thinking of a woman he once knew.

"You can't do that," Meggy replied, squeezing the ball.

"Exactly. But the girl was so thirsty and so afraid that she didn't dare question him. She squeezed and squeezed the stone, but no water came out. Dogma told the girl that if she believed, it would. So the girl squeezed and squeezed and believed and believed. Still, no water came out."

"What happened then?"

"At that very moment, a knight of truth appeared, wielding a glowing sword, and Dogma took flight as fast as he could. The knight asked the girl why she was squeezing a stone, and she revealed what Dogma had told her. The knight told the girl that there was no water in the stone, and the girl rued her foolishness.

"The knight approached, and told the girl that being fooled did not make her foolish: that all who drew breath could be fooled, from kings to stable hands, scholars to laborers—even Dogma himself. The knight's helm opened and bloomed into a cloth hat, the shimmering armor beneath it into a muddy gray robe, and the glowing sword into a moss-covered staff.

"The sorceress, an old but strong woman, asked if the girl was still thirsty, and offered to take her to a place that would quench her thirst. Fearing the unknown lands ahead, the girl asked how the two of them would find their way without a map. 'Reason and truth will be our guide,' the sorceress replied, 'and your heart will be the compass.'

"The girl found the courage to join the sorceress, and before long, they came upon the shore of a great lake. The girl drank until she thirsted no more, and in time, the sorceress carved her her own staff, bidding her travel on alone. The girl set sail to find all the lakes and oceans in the world—and if you have compassion in your heart and the courage to face the truth, maybe, just maybe, you might end up meeting her. The end."

Meggy looked up, puzzled. "That's it?"

"That's it."

"I don't get it."

"I didn't at first. To be honest, neither did my dad. You see, love is like water. If you want it, you have to go where it is. Some people are like lakes because they have so much love to give you. And some are like rocks—no matter what you do or how much you give them, they won't love you back. Go where the water is, and you'll always find what you need."

"Tom?"

"Yes?"

"Are you where the water is?"

Tom's heart ached as he looked back at Meggy. "I'm... a pond."

"A pond?"

"Just a pond. It's okay to occasionally get water from a pond, but lakes and oceans have much more to offer you. Promise me you'll always go where the water is, and you'll make me happier than any drawing."

"But does that mean I won't see you again?"

"Of course not. Bolingbrook is a small place. But I'm giving you permission to spend more time with the lakes and oceans. Promise?"

Meggy grabbed Tom's waist and hugged him again. "Promise."

A notification popped up on the desktop. Tom disconnected the tablet and returned it to her.

"Next time someone asks you to download something, ask your parents' permission. Always."

Meggy nodded, "I will."

"You might want to go check in with them now."

"Off to the lakes!"

Tom chuckled. "Come on then. I'll let you out."

Tom escorted Meggy to the shop door.

"I have a question," said Meggy.

"Sure."

"At my Sunday school, God is in every story. Where was He in the stable girl's?"

Tom smiled. "Her world is all there is, and all she needs."

Meggy gave Tom a sidelong glance. "Your Sunday school is weird."

***

Tom adjusted his tie in the rear-view mirror, then looked out at the *Babbler's* office. Not long ago, he'd wanted to drive them out of business. Now he wanted nothing more than to work for them.

Tom collected his folder, then stepped out of the car, waving at Wendy as she appeared in the parking lot.

"Good to see you again," she said.

"Good to be back," Tom replied. "I hope the outfit's okay. I haven't worn it in ages."

"Looks fine. How's the ear?"

"Better now, thanks."

"You must have really ticked Robert off for him to use a slow extraction on you. That's the most painful way."

"There's a less painful way?"

"Several, in fact."

Tom winced. "I gotta go. Don't want to miss my shot."

"Good luck."

"Any advice?"

"Just remember: no matter how it goes, you learned from this."

"And survived."

Wendy nodded.

Tom entered the office and saw staffers rushing between desks and cubicles. It reminded him of his days at UIC. Years ago, he'd given up hope of ever working inside a newsroom again. Had he inadvertently earned another chance?

Tom heard Jenna talking over the phone before spotting her at her desk. She noticed him and waved, then pointed to her earpiece. "I already added the picture. Yes, the red one." She nodded again. "No, thank *you*. Goodbye."

Jenna tapped her headset, then rushed to the counter.

"Sorry about that," she said as she lifted the bar top, letting Tom through. "It gets hectic on deadline day."

"Did I just see you using your powers?"

"No, I've just worked with him long enough to know what he wants."

Jenna escorted Tom to Sara's cubicle, where he sat down in the guest chair.

"She'll be with you soon." Jenna turned away.

"Jenna?"

"Yes?"

"Can you tell me how this goes? I mean, if I end up here?"

Jenna shrugged. "All I can tell you is you're on a single path now."

"Just one?"

"Just one."

As Jenna smiled and left, Tom placed his folder on the desk, preparing for his interview. "Run this by Wendy," he heard Sara say moments later, and stood as she entered.

"Thank you for coming in on short notice."

Tom shook her hand. "Thank you for considering me."

Sara sat at her desk, and Tom, following her lead, sat as well.

"You really told Robert you were on assignment for us?" Tom nodded. "Few would have said that to him," Sara smiled. "A point in your favor."

Tom pushed his folder across Sara's desk. "If you need more clips, I brought these."

"Your cover story is all I needed to see. Now." Sara cleared her throat. "This is about the staff reporter position. No special perks—we won't provide you with a web domain or blog. You'll have your choice of an open desk or a cubicle. I enjoyed your last post, by the way. I take it it means I won't have to worry about you and Jamie Kyle?"

"Absolutely. We're not friends, but we'll coexist for now. I also meant it when I said I never want to go back down that path. I've been doing a lot of reading, but I'll learn whatever I need to."

"Good to hear. I don't expect you to earn a PhD, but I do expect my staffers to know what they're writing about. And if we hire you, you'll be expected to act professionally at all times. Understood?"

Tom nodded.

"This won't be like writing for your blog. Many readers won't believe your stories. Sometimes you might be heckled in public. That'll be in addition to the trolling you're receiving from your former friends right now."

"It's a taste of what I did to others. Nowhere near as bad as what Jamie and Sakura deal with."

"You're catching on. Now, do you have any questions?"

"What advice do you have for a junior reporter?"

"Advice?" Sara stood and approached Tom, who looked up at her. "Before I joined the *Babbler*, somebody offered me a chance to walk away. He said I was about to go down a dangerous path. Working here was right for me, but it might not be for you. You won't succeed here if you have any doubts, Tom. So look around. Is this where you belong?"

Tom stood and looked around the *Babbler* newsroom. Framed copies of past issues hung on the brick walls, one headline reading *MARTIAN COLONIES SIGN PEACE TREATY WITH BOLINGBROOK*. Tom guessed it must have been published a week or two after he'd first watched Reese's DVD. "I've given this a lot of thought," he said, "and this is where I want to be."

"Why is that?"

Tom considered his words, glancing at the newsroom walls. "At the Golf Club, Robert offered me the chance to be his village skeptic. I decided I didn't feel like being part of his machine. Bennett made me an offer too—something about leading the middle way between sexism and feminism. I don't know if I still think that exists. Even if I did, I'm done covering for him.

"When I was a kid, I loved the *Babbler*. Every issue made me want to learn more about this town. I wanted to know all about Martian Colonies and vampire gangs. I wanted to find out the truth. Reese and my dad thought they were doing me a favor when they started me down the path of skepticism, but that wasn't the path for me. I shouldn't have needed to see my future to understand that. Now when I look around these walls, I see the truth.

"Reading the *Babbler* used to make me feel like I was home. It was my home. But I wandered away too long ago. Being here feels like I've found my way back." Tom felt his eyes water as he looked at Sara. "I'd like to come home, please."

Sara nodded, then picked up Tom's folder. "Wait here," she said. For several long minutes, Tom listened to the buzz of activity from outside the cubicle.

"Tom?" asked Jenna, popping her head in. "Come with me." Tom stood and followed her into the open area.

"Everyone!" she announced. "May I have your attention please?" The room gradually quieted as the staff focused on Jenna and Tom. "I'd like for all of you to meet Tom Larsen." She gestured at Tom. "He's been through quite a journey to join us."

"That guy?" remarked one staffer in disgust.

"Yeah," Wendy answered. "That guy. He's earned it."

Jenna dramatically turned towards Tom. "Last chance. Do you still want to join?"

"Yes," Tom replied, trying to sound calm and professional.

Sara stepped out of the publisher's office with a worn yellow and white phone book. Tom hadn't seen one like it since he'd visited his grandparents years earlier.

"Tom," said Jenna dramatically. "When my grandfather founded the *Babbler*, he asked all the reporters to take an oath to the village residents. It's become a tradition for all new reporters to take it."

Sara approached with the phone book. "Raise your right hand, and place your left hand on the book." Tom did. "Tom," asked Sara. "Do you swear or affirm that you will tell the truth to the people of Bolingbrook, no matter how unbelievable it might be?"

"I do," said Tom.

"Do you also promise not to deceive the residents of Bolingbrook?"

"I do," he said.

"Do you understand that violating this oath may lead to your termination?"

"I do."

"Then by the power granted to me by Olson Family Media LLC, I, Editor Sara Langston, am offering you a staff reporter position at the *Bolingbrook Babbler*. Do you accept?"

"I do," said Tom, smiling proudly.

Sara offered her hand. "Welcome home, Tom."

The End

***

Tom returns in Revenge of the Phantom Press.

Thank You

Thank you for reading this book. If you liked it, please consider leaving a review at Goodreads and/or where you obtained a copy. Even a single sentence review could encourage someone to get a copy.

For updates about my writing, and bonus stories, please subscribe to my newsletter.

Mailing List: bolingbrookbabbler.com/sign-up-for-the-bolingbrook-babbler-newsletter-2/

Fiction Blog: freethoughtblogs.com/babbler

Author Page: www.bolingbrookbabbler.com

g
goodreads.com/author/show/5699299.William_Brinkman

f
facebook.com/bolingbrookbabbler/

♪
tiktok.com/@williambrinkmanbb

Acknowledgments

First off, thanks to my editor for their hard work and for helping me on my journey to becoming a novelist.

Thanks to my beta readers for their valuable comments, which helped me add depth to this story.

Thanks to my wife for her support and feedback. It's hard to believe that I started on this book before we got married.

Thanks to *Freethought Blogs* for accepting me into the network. I've learned so much as a member.

Thanks to the residents of Bolingbrook for inspiring me over the years. Living in Bolingbrook marked a transition for me, and it will always have a place in my heart.

Finally, the arc of history does not bend towards justice, and social progress isn't pulled by the magical hand of civilization. It takes work to make it happen. Thanks to the people fighting to create a better and just world, regardless of religious beliefs, or non-belief.

About William Brinkman

In William Brinkman's world, suburban sidewalks lead to secret conspiracies, emotional reckonings, and the occasional enraged weredeer. He writes urban fantasy with a blend of satire and heart, offering humanistic views of the real world through a supernatural lens. Since 1999, he's published the Bolingbrook Babbler blog, which inspired—but remains separate from—his fiction. His book, *A Fire in the Shadows*, made the short list for the 2024 Indieverse Award for Best Novella. A former Bolingbrook resident, William now lives in suburban Chicagoland with his wife and two cats.

For updates and a free eBook, *God to Smite Bolingbrook*, sign up for his newsletter.

https://bolingbrookbabbler.com/mailing-list

g

goodreads.com/author/show/5699299.William_Brinkman

f

facebook.com/bolingbrookbabbler/

♪

tiktok.com/@williambrinkmanbb

Also By William Brinkman

The Bolingbrook Babbler Stories
- *Pathways to Bolingbrook: A Bolingbrook Babbler Story* Book 1 (2021)

- *A Fire in the Shadows: A Bolingbrook Babbler Story Book 1.5 (2023)*

- *The Rift: A Bolingbrook Babbler Story* Book 2 (2022)

- *Revenge of the Phantom Press: A Bolingbrook Babbler Story* Book 3 (2026)

Web Fiction Collection
- God to Smite Bolingbrook (2023)

Demon: The Fallen (White Wolf Studios)
- *Demon: The Fallen* (2002)

- *Saviors and Destroyers* "Broken Bonds" (2003)

- *Damned and Deceived* "The Good Soldier"

(2003)

www.ingramcontent.com/pod-product-compliance
Lightning Source LLC
Chambersburg PA
CBHW030806020726
47499CB00006B/1791